THE MITCHELLS: FIVE FOR VICTORY

The Mitchells:
Five for Victory

WRITTEN AND ILLUSTRATED BY
Hilda van Stockum

BETHLEHEM BOOKS • IGNATIUS PRESS
WARSAW, NORTH DAKOTA
1995

Originally published by
The Viking Press, 1945

Reprint edition

Special features © 1995 Bethlehem Books

All Rights Reserved

ISBN 1-883937-05-1

Library of Congress Catalogue number: 94-79549

Cover art by Hilda van Stockum

Cover Design by Davin Carlson

Bethlehem Books • Ignatius Press
R.R. 1 Box 137-A
Minto, ND 58261
Printed in the United States of America

TO MY BELOVED BROTHER WILLEM
AND TO ALL OTHERS
WHO LAID DOWN THEIR LIVES
FOR THEIR FRIENDS

Contents

The Mitchells: Five for Victory

ONE

Father Leaves

IN THE hot July sun Washington's Union Station seemed like a vaulted oven. Joan felt the heat more than the other Mitchell children because she rushed around so. She could see little sweat drops glistening on her nose when she shut one eye. She tried it first on the left side and then on the right. It made her forget about Daddy. Joan hated "good-bys" and this one was going to be terrible, worse even than when Uncle Jim had left. Daddy hadn't been drafted very long yet, and the Mitchells had hoped he would have a long period of training first, like Uncle Jim. But the Navy needed electrical engineers so badly that they had made Daddy a lieutenant right away and after a few weeks' training he had been assigned to a ship. Now his family was seeing him off.

A lot of other people seemed to be leaving at the same time as Daddy. The station was full of uniforms, weeping ladies and shrieking children. Joan hoped Mother wouldn't cry. She knew Grannie would, but Grannie was so old Joan felt sure people would understand and forgive her. Besides, there were strangers who were sobbing too, and Joan appeared to be the only one who blushed for them. One soldier had to take leave of a dog, and the dog didn't understand. He was a strong dog and he was dragging a red-eyed lady around on a leash. When the soldier tried to rush past the ticket collector, the dog gave a howl and bounded after him, tripping up Daddy with the leash. Luckily Daddy was able to catch his balance in midair.

"Dogs!" he muttered in a tone of rage. Daddy hated dogs.

"I'm so sorry," began the lady on the leash, but the dog didn't wait for her to finish. He whisked her off and she soon vanished in the crowd.

"Dogs!" repeated Father, almost sounding like one himself, he growled so. "Useless parasites of civilization, objects of slobbering sentimentality, verminous vandals. . . ."

"Daddy, don't say such bad words!" cried Joan, shocked. Daddy's blue eyes twinkled down on her.

"Joan," he said, "I know you and I warn you. Don't you go filling my house with animals while I'm gone. I don't want to come back to a *zoo!* And especially, *no dogs!* Do you hear?"

"Yes, Daddy," said Joan meekly, though with a heavy heart. Joan loved animals and longed for a pet, but Daddy

said five children were noise, confusion and expense
enough.

"Hurry, John!" cried Mother, who was trying to keep
her youngest daughter from being trampled underfoot.
"We're late!"

Joan's heart skipped a beat. What if Daddy missed the
train and let the ship go off without him? Would he be
courtmartialed? They were very strict in the Navy.

"Daddy! Daddy! Hurry!" she cried, tugging at his uniform.

But Daddy was as calm as ever. Now they were shoving
past the ticket collector and there beside the platform
stood the train, panting to leave. Lieutenant Mitchell
took a hasty farewell of his family. First Grannie, then
Mother, who held Baby Timmy, then Joan, Patsy, Peter
and Angela. The train was already in motion when he
jumped on, his cap at a rakish angle.

"Don't forget your gun!" shouted Peter after him. "And
shoot first, hear?"

"And bring back a baby-orphan from Europe!" yelled
Patsy. Daddy was already too far off to hear, which was
just as well, thought Mother. She had enough children to
take care of at present.

"You take Peter and Patsy, Grannie, will you?" she
said. "And watch out for those luggage carts. Joan! You
hold Angela."

Another train thundered into the station, oozing pas-
sengers, who pushed past Mother and unsettled her
pretty new hat with the red cherries. It dropped over one
ear, giving Mother a wild look as she clutched Timmy and
tried to watch over the other children as well.

"Take care!" she cried, but Joan had already caught
Angela before the child could fall off the platform.

Angela was the beauty of the family and she had need to be, as Mother often remarked grimly. If she hadn't been so cherubic, with long blond curls, wistful blue eyes and the most enchanting little legs in the whole wide world, she'd surely have been disowned long ago! She was more trouble than the rest of the family put together. Now she set up a howl as Joan attempted to force her to follow the family procession.

"My shoe!" she screamed. "My li'l shoe!" Joan looked down. Yes—Angela was walking on one sock and one shoe.

"Mother! Mother!" cried Joan. "Wait!" Mother heard her, notwithstanding the roar and rumble of traffic.

"What is it?" she asked, turning around.

"Angela has lost her shoe."

"Oh my goodness," sighed Mother. "And I've spent my last shoe stamp. We'll just have to find it." She gazed around at the shuffling crowd.

"Grannie!" she cried. Grannie had gone on, not noticing the interruption, but Peter pulled her to a standstill.

"Mother is calling you."

"Yes, what?" said Grannie. She was thinking of Daddy and it was hard to make her understand.

"Shoe? Which shoe?" she asked.

"Never mind," said Mother. "You go on with Peter and Patsy; we'll find you in the waiting room. I've got to hurry and look for that shoe."

So Grannie walked on with her portion of the Mitchell family, while Mother straightened her hat, settled Timmy firmly on her arm and ran back to Joan and Angela, who each wanted to go in a different direction. Poor Joan's face looked like a radish.

"It's no use," she cried bitterly. "I can't do a *thing* with her." And with melancholy eyes she watched a bead of sweat roll down her nose and jump off at the tip.

"My shoe!" cried Angela in a heartbroken voice. "The pretty li'l one!"

"Where did you lose it?" asked Mother, peering around in vain.

"Down there," said Angela, pointing a fat little finger at the tracks. "I threw him."

"You threw it?" cried Mother indignantly. Joan couldn't help laughing, and after casting an angry look at her, Mother had to laugh, too. The little white shoe perched jauntily on one of the gleaming steel tracks.

"How shall we ever get it back?" sighed Mother.

"Why don't you ask a porter?" suggested Joan.

"I see one there," and she was off, presently returning with a redcap, who took in the situation at once.

"I'll have it for you in a jiffy, ma'am," he promised, lowering himself to the tracks while Joan watched anxiously for possible trains. The porter picked up the shoe, dusted it on his sleeve, and leaped back on to the platform with astonishing agility.

"Now don't go losing it again, honey," he told Angela as he bent to put the shoe back on her foot. Angela rewarded him with a golden smile. The porter flashed his teeth at her and straightened up again.

"Lawdy, ma'am!" he cried, rolling his eyes and pointing at Timmy, who sat still as an angel on Mother's arm. "That chile is eating your hat!" Mother hastily lowered Timmy to look at him. The baby gazed back at her complacently, his face smeared with red paint. In his hands he held the pretty bunch of imitation cherries, several of them obviously missing.

"Goodness, I hope they're not poisonous!" cried Mother, trying to clean Timmy's face with her handkerchief.

The redcap laughed. "I don't reckon so, ma'am," he murmured consolingly. "They're just paper and paint; he'll never notice it. It was your hat I was thinking of, such a pretty hat, too. Give me the boy, I'll tote him for you; you look plumb tuckered out." And the good-natured porter took Timmy and put him on his shoulder. Timmy gazed triumphantly down on Mother.

"That *is* a relief," sighed Mother gratefully, fanning herself with her plucked hat.

"Where were you all fixing to go?" asked the redcap.

"To the waiting room," said Mother, hurrying to keep up with his long strides. "I have more children there, waiting with my mother-in-law."

"Whew!" whistled the porter. "How are you all going to get home?"

"In a taxi, I suppose," said Mother wearily. She

couldn't face the long bus journey after all this. It meant changing into another bus, half-way, too.

"You'll need a moving van," the redcap told her. He pushed ahead, Timmy crowing with delight at seeing so much of the world. Mother and Joan followed, with Angela between them.

When they arrived at the spacious waiting room with its ocean of seats, Mother asked: "Do you see Grannie anywhere?" Joan peered around.

"No," she said.

"I wonder where she went?" murmured Mother.

"There's a lady's waiting room further on," the porter pointed out helpfully. "Perhaps she went there."

"Yes . . ." said Mother. "That will be it," and she made a motion to go on, but Joan had caught sight of a glass counter and cried:

"Oh! Look at the lovely toys!"

"Hush!" cried Mother warningly, but it was too late, Angela had heard.

"Which toys?" she cried, pulling herself loose and streaking off in the direction Joan had pointed.

"Oh dear, I'm sorry," said Joan. Mother shrugged her shoulders. It couldn't be helped, and slowly they followed Angela, who was already squatting on the floor before the counter, wrapped in bliss.

"Oh! see? Look at the pussy, oh, the *sweet* pussy! Oh Mommy, Mommy, I want the pussy! I want that pussy, Mommy, that *cute* li'l pussy!" Angela jumped to her feet again and skipped up and down in a frenzy of joy, her curls flying, her eyes blazing blue fire.

"How much is it?" Mother asked timidly of a very superior lady who sat behind the counter, slowly chewing gum with an air as if the toys were no concern of hers.

"Oh, that . . ." she said, looking down her nose at the true-to-life fur kitten of Angela's choice.

"Two-ninety-eight," she announced.

Mother was aghast. "For *that* little thing?"

"Oh, Mother, buy it for her!" pleaded Joan. "She likes it so much."

"But I can't," said Mother wildly, remembering the few dollar bills in her slender purse which still had to yield the taxi's fare as well as the porter's tip. "I just *can't.*"

Angela looked incredulous. She couldn't have that pussy? Unbelievable! She sat down on the ground and started a howl which seemed to come from the toes of her little feet, winding its way through her chubby body and exploding from her rosy lips with the force of a blackout siren. Even the lady behind the counter stopped chewing and took notice.

"She can't do that here," she remarked in an injured voice, frowning down on what she could see of Angela through two layers of glass.

"Oh, can't she?" echoed Mother bitterly.

But Joan had already taken the matter in hand. Seemingly heedless of Angela, she studied the pussycat with cold disdain.

"I don't like that pussy," she said loudly. "I bet it can't walk, or scratch, or mew, or even purr." Angela stopped screaming and listened. She had been disappointed in toys before. Was this pussy, perhaps, not as perfect as it seemed?

"It is, too, a neat pussy," she said defiantly.

But Joan perceived that her words had taken effect. "Santa Claus has much neater pussies . . ." she began. "And look . . . there's Grannie!" Yes, there was Grannie, who had waxed impatient and had sallied forth, re-

membering that Mother might have meant the general
waiting room after all.

"Oh, I'm so glad you're all right," she cried, seeing the
little group before the glass counter. "I was afraid something had happened to you."

"And I," began Mother, but she was interrupted by
shrieks from Peter and Patsy, who had discovered the
toys, while Angela ran to her grandmother and poured out
her woes.

"Mommy won't buy the li'l pussy," she said, pointing
to the kitten.

"Oh, I'll pay for it," said Grannie immediately, opening
her bag.

"Grannie dear, you mustn't," cried Mother, alarmed.
"It's two-ninety-eight."

"Buy *me* something, buy *me* something," cried Peter,
Patsy and Joan, dancing around like wild Indians.

"Don't you all want a taxi now?" asked the porter,
growing impatient at last. But Grannie had approached
the glass counter, fumbling with her purse, and Mother
sighed.

"You'd better give the baby to me if you are in a hurry,"
she told the porter. "I can see we won't be through here
for some time. Please, Mother," she begged, laying a hand
on Grannie's shoulder, "Don't ruin yourself. Let me pay
for this; I can take it out of next month's allowance."

But Grannie was stubborn. "I don't have to go to the
hairdresser now John and Jim have both left," she said.
"I'll wash my own hair and be rich." Mother couldn't say
anything after that, for Angela had grabbed her pussy and
run away with it like a dog with a bone, doubtless fearing
that Grannie might change her mind. She was half-way
down the huge room before Mother caught up with her.

"I want candy," she announced as her eyes lit on a slot-machine. Mother got her some.

"It's all wrong," she thought. "The child is being spoilt, but we've got to get home some time," and she walked quickly back with a now radiant Angela.

Grannie was sitting triumphantly on a bench with Timmy on her lap. The redcap had gone and the other children were blissful with presents. Joan and Patsy had each chosen a children's magazine and Peter was zooming a little wooden airplane about.

"I paid for everything," crowed Grannie, "even for the porter."

"You shouldn't have done it," murmured Mother, but she felt relieved and began to cheer up. "Come along, chickens," she said. "Peter, don't fly that plane, it might hit someone."

But Peter had already let it go and it did hit someone, a fat gentleman who looked annoyed and crushed it with his foot. Peter picked up the wreck and wept over it. The other children gathered around to mourn with him.

"Come along," cried Mother. "I still have to cook dinner! It was your own fault, Peter. I told you not to fly it here, it's too dangerous."

"I *had* to," Peter defended himself. "In a war you can't just stay home because it's safer!"

"Perhaps that man was an anti-aircraft gun," suggested Patsy.

"No, he looked more like a barrage balloon," remarked Joan.

"Yes," agreed Peter, and a smile shone through his tears. He lovingly wrapped the remains of his plane in his handkerchief, with a vague idea of "gluing" them when he got home.

"Come, children!" cried Mother from afar. "We have to get a taxi!"

"A taxi? Are we going in a taxi? Oh boy!" And the children ran like hounds after a scent.

"May I sit in front? May I? May I?"

"Peter may," Mother decided, "because he was good about his wrecked plane."

They still had to find a taxi, however. There was a crowd waiting and there weren't enough taxis to go around. People had to double up. But, as Joan remarked, the Mitchells were double already, and when they at last had their taxi they filled it completely. Peter and Patsy were squeezed in front with the driver, congratulating each other on their luck.

"*We* see all the *new* things, and in the back they see only *old* things," Patsy summed up. Then they took the driver into their confidence and told him that their Daddy had gone to the war.

"Why don't *you* go to the war?" asked Patsy. "You're a man, too."

"They won't have me," grumbled the taxi driver. "I'm too old."

"Oh." The children looked at him. He *did* look rather old with wrinkles in his face and whitish kind of hair. Not as white as Grannie's, but white as a spider's web. Grannie's was white as a Christmas tree angel.

"It's like me," said Peter. "I'm too young." The taxi driver's face grew still more wrinkled as he gave Peter a sideways glance.

"I guess you are, at that," he admitted. "How old *are* you?"

"Six," said Peter. "And anyway, I've to look after my family."

"Oh," said the driver. "You've a family, have you?"

"Well, all of us," explained Peter, sweeping his arm around and hitting Patsy in the face. Patsy protested, but Peter paid no attention.

"I'm the only man in the family, the only one that can *talk*. It's a big . . . a big . . . what was the word Daddy said, Patsy?"

"I don't care," sulked Patsy. "You hit me."

"Well, anyway," Peter went on hurriedly, "I've a lot of expendents."

"Dependents, you mean," chuckled the taxi driver. "Or is it expenses?" Peter thought it better to let it go. That was the trouble with new words—they were very attractive, but people were always asking what they meant.

"Daddy had to go to the war because people were making so many mistakes," he explained, changing the subject.

"Yes," said Patsy. "I guess we'll win soon now."

"It can't be too soon for me," sighed the taxi driver. "I've got two sons in Italy."

They were nearing Chevy Chase circle and soon the children cried:

"Here we are! Here we are!" as the taxi stopped in front of a comfortable stucco house, which looked rather the worse for wear. Several dolls and a toy gun lay scattered over the front steps. While Mother paid the driver Grannie lifted Timmy out and the other children stumbled on to the sidewalk without assistance. The house looked cold and empty, and Joan remembered that it was Cora the maid's day off.

She skipped up the steps and went to open the door. She pulled at it and pushed and kicked. She rattled the knob. It wouldn't open. Patsy and Peter came and pushed and rattled and kicked, too, but it didn't help. The door was definitely locked. Oh, well! They ran to the back door and tried it. No, sir, locked, too. Then they went to the cellar door. Also locked. Joan thought this must be the very first time since they lived in the house that all the doors were locked at the same time. The children ran back to the front again. Mother was coming up the steps, loaded with Timmy, and Grannie came puffing after her.

"The doors are locked!" cried Peter.

"Oh!" Mother sat down on a step and tried to open her bag while balancing Timmy on her knee.

"I'll take him," said Joan eagerly, grasping her fat little brother in her strong arms and lifting him up.

"Oh dear," cried Mother, rummaging frantically through her bag and scattering ration books, fountain pen,

spectacles, stamps and letters around her. "Oh dear, how stupid, how ridiculous—whatever *shall* we do?"

"What is it, Mother?" cried the children. Mother looked ready to burst into tears. She wiped her forehead, pushing her hat back, the sorry hat without its cherries, and glanced up at the closed house.

"Oh, nothing," she sighed. "Only—Daddy has the key."

TWO

Changes

I F ALL misfortunes were like missing a latch key,
thought Joan, the world would be a merry place. It
didn't take her and Peter long to climb from the mulberry
tree to the porch roof and from there through a pried-
open window. It was much harder to get used to missing
Daddy. A day without Daddy was like a sentence without capital letter or period. The mornings seemed empty
without the hum of his electric razor and his stentorian
calls for "a clean towel" or "some soap, for Heaven's
sake!"

The first morning after Daddy had left, Peter went to
the bathroom door and began to rattle the knob as usual,

with a wail of "let me in!" To his surprise the door flew open and he fell headlong on the tiles, bumping his nose. Then he remembered that it would be a long time before he could dress himself again while watching Daddy shave.

At dinnertime Mother now sat at Daddy's place, looking plump and harassed after Daddy's lean, deft ways. It was funny to see her carve the meat. When Daddy did it, it seemed easy. He never even pulled a face. He only looked quiet and masterful, and his sharp knife, which he'd beat up a couple of times if it wouldn't behave, slid meekly through the meat, carving it in thin, polite slices. When you got one on your plate you knew here was a piece of meat that knew its place and would do as it was told, without nonsense. It almost whispered: "Excuse me," when your knife happened to slip. But Mother's helpings were quite different. They were fractious lumps of the oddest shapes, which turned their backs on you when they got the chance and loved to escape from under your knife or slip off your plate. When at last you had captured a mouthful it was sure to be all gristle. Watching Mother carve was as good as a movie. When it went well she'd flush and beam with pride. Then, suddenly, she'd frown and mutter things and wrestle with the meat as though it were an intractable child.

"Stop it!" she'd cry furiously, to the exquisite delight of her brood. Mother said the meat had got worse and it wasn't her fault. But Joan didn't believe a word of it. No meat would ever have *dared* behave like that with Daddy!

Meals were more adventurous without him but less nourishing.

But it was on Sundays that the children missed their father most. He used to take them for drives in the country, and when gasoline rationing had put an end to that, he had taken them for walks instead. They had explored all the "for sale" and "for rent" signs in the neighborhood. Daddy collected houses the way other people collect stamps, and he was always talking about buying one. Mother said it was a mercy he had no money, for if he ever owned a house, where would his hobby be?

The children agreed with Daddy that it was fun to visit empty houses and pretend you were going to live in them. They knew almost all the houses in the street that way and had given them nicknames. There was the "Curlicue House," with its elaborate ornament; the "Haunted House," never occupied for long; the "Dreary House," which had nothing whatever to recommend it; and, last but not least, the "White Elephant." The "White Elephant" was a huge white house with a large yard. Probably it had once been a country estate, but now the city had overtaken it, busses roared past it. Shops stared it out of countenance, and its blockful of nature looked out of place. The children called it the "White Elephant" because Daddy had once said that it would take a lot of money to keep up and was a "white elephant" on the market. Joan had immediately inquired the meaning of that expression and the explanation had puzzled her. It seemed strange that people didn't want white elephants. She would have *loved* one, especially if its ears were pink inside, like those of white rabbits. She'd be sure to be fonder of a white elephant than of anything else in the world, but no one had ever offered her one.

Meanwhile it was just as well that nobody wanted the big white house. It was the only place where they could play "Red Indians," "Pioneers," or "Christopher Columbus" to their hearts' content. It was full of knotty, climbable trees, dense evergreens, long tangled grass, ivy and wild berries. Besides, it boasted a *playhouse*. To be sure, the paint had worn off, the glass had vanished from the windows, and the door now wobbled drunkenly on one rusty hinge, but it still served to play "house" in, or to imprison captive Red Indians. So far as Joan was concerned the place could remain a "White Elephant" forever.

Mother had seldom accompanied Daddy and the children on these trips. She said that after she worried over the shape of an empty house and tried to imagine how her furniture would fit inside it, she felt as tired as if she had actually moved, so she preferred to stay home, thank you. There was little chance therefore of visiting empty houses while Daddy was away. There weren't many left of them now, anyway. It was almost two years after Pearl Harbor and people were still pouring into the Capital to help win the war. Three empty houses in the street had been taken, including the "Haunted House," but that was sure to be for rent again soon. The children believed it harbored a ghost who chased all occupants away. Luckily the "White Elephant" wasn't taken yet, though the papers were full of jokes about the lack of living space in Washington; there were even pictures of people sleeping in bathtubs. The White Elephant had lots of rooms as well as three bathrooms of its own.

"Well, what do we care," asked Peter "as long as we can play there?"

The children needed the extra space, for Mother had plowed up most of their yard to make a victory garden, leaving only a fenced-in place for Timmy. Of course, having a victory garden was fun, too. The children took a personal pride in the height of their corn and the size of their tomatoes. It was also a comfort to know that there would at least be *something* to eat if worse came to worst. More food was being rationed all the time and for a while there hadn't been any potatoes and now there was no butter. But the children daren't grumble for fear Mother and Grannie would get angry. Grannie had come from Holland as a young girl and she still had friends and relatives over there. When Joan once complained that she had nothing to eat because she didn't like oatmeal and despised margarine, Grannie grew pale, with flashing eyes, and Mother grew red and shouted, but it amounted to the same thing:

Children in Europe were starving. A little girl had been flung into prison by the Nazis because she had spilt some of that very oatmeal. The bread in Holland was made of bulbs and gave you a stomach-ache. Babies were dying because the milk was mostly water. Peter and Patsy promptly offered their food to the poor little children, only to be told that it could not be sent, after which Joan wanted to know what difference it made, in that case, whether they liked their food or didn't, and whether it wasn't mean to be so pleased with what others couldn't have. Then Mother and Grannie started to argue about that. Grannie said that she felt like Joan; you couldn't be enjoying yourself while others were suffering; but Mother insisted that while there was so much misery in the world, which couldn't be helped, one ought at least to be happy whenever one could.

"And grumbling is *always* wrong, Joan," she ended severely. "So blow your nose and keep still."

Joan often wondered what she should do if the enemy ever came near. Of course, that wasn't possible. Not with Daddy's ship protecting them. But it had happened to other people. Joan couldn't imagine strange soldiers ever *daring* to break into her home to kill her family. She was glad the enemy was so far away and that Daddy was helping to keep him there.

At bedtime Mother always came to tuck the children in and that was the moment of the day Joan loved best. Then she could ask any question she liked and delay the odious hour when she would have to put her ear on the pillow and surrender to sleep.

"Is Uncle Jim braver than Daddy?" she asked one night.

"No, of course not, what makes you think so?" asked Mother, shocked.

"Well, he enlisted right after Pearl Harbor and Daddy waited until now," explained Joan.

"Oh, but, my dear, Uncle Jim had no one else to worry about while Daddy has all of you as well as Grannie and me."

"Why didn't Uncle Jim marry like Daddy?" asked Patsy.

"I guess he didn't find the right person," said Mother.

"It must be awfully hard to find one," sighed Joan. "How did you get Daddy?"

"My goodness," laughed Mother. "I'll tell you that another time, when it isn't so late."

"Don't go away yet," cried the girls, clutching their mother. "We want to hear *lots* more."

"I'll get so I won't dare come up here," said Mother, pretending to be scared. "Will you come into my parlor said the spider to the fly. . . . I've got two spiders here."

"Yes, we're spiders," yelled Patsy. "I'm eating you!" She and Joan almost strangled Mother with their strong arms.

"Stop it, stop it!" cried Mother, wrenching herself free.

"You're not spiders, you're boa constrictors. Lie down! Both of you!" The girls heard a warning note in Mother's voice and crawled under their sheets. But Patsy still ventured to say:

"How do you think a spider would look to a fly?" Joan shuddered. "Don't talk of it," she cried.

"Good night, girls," said Mother. "Remember! Not a sound!"

Joan shut her eyes. Mother's footsteps went down and grew fainter. Soon all was still. Joan opened her eyes. A twig of leaves moved in front of the lantern outside, throwing huge shadows on the wall in the attic room. Joan sat up.

"Pst! Patsy!" she whispered.

"What?"

"I've been wondering. Do you think *we* could do something to help win the war?"

"I think we ought to help Mother," said Patsy. "She doesn't laugh half as often as when Daddy was here. She is always writing figures and looking worried."

"I guess she doesn't have as much money," Joan murmured thoughtfully.

"Sh! I hear someone coming!" And the girls dived under their sheets. But it was only Peter in his pajamas.

"What are you doing here?" asked Joan.

"Oh, just visiting," explained Peter, crouching at the foot end of Joan's bed and playing with his toes. "It's too hot to sleep and I heard you talking."

"Gosh, did Mother hear us?"

"Oh no. She's downstairs doing arithmetic," Peter reassured her. "I looked over the banisters. What are you talking about?"

"About Mother. We think she is a lot poorer now Daddy

is in the Navy and prices have gone up too. I think we ought to help Mother make things last. I have a lovely plan."

"What plan?" asked the others eagerly.

"I think we ought to have a club. We're a rather special family, you know."

"Why?" asked Patsy.

"There are five of us," Joan told her, "and you know what five looks like on the clock, don't you?"

"V for Victory!" cried Peter.

"Yes, and we ought to be Victory children and help win the war by earning war stamps and saving scrap. That way we'll bring Daddy back quickly."

"Yes," said Patsy. "But then Angela and Timmy have to help too or there won't be five of us, and what can they do?"

"Timmy helps already, in a way, because he makes Mother laugh," Joan told her.

"But Angela?" asked Patsy. "What can Angela do?" That was a problem indeed. The children thought and thought, but the more they remembered Angela's character the less faith they had in any aid from her.

"She could save all her naughtiness until after the war," Peter proposed at last.

"She'd never remember. You don't know little children," Joan told him. At last they decided that Angela and Timmy would be regarded as mascots. Meanwhile they could ask two of their friends to join as active members.

"Dickie!" cried Peter immediately. Dickie was his bosom friend.

"And Tilly," said Joan. Tilly was the new girl who had just come to live in the haunted house. She was the only girl of Joan's age in the neighborhood.

"Now we'll have to write down the rules . . ." began Joan. "Put on the light, Patsy . . ." But before Patsy could reach for the cord there were terrible sounds downstairs which told them that Mother had discovered Peter's empty bed. Peter almost tumbled down the steps in his hurry to appease his angry parent, but she managed to get in a hard slap on the seat of his pajamas before he ducked under his bedsheet, leaving only a lock of hair to face Mother's wrath. When she had told Peter forcibly what she thought of children who went visiting after they had been put to bed, Mother went up the stairs to the attic room. She found the place dark and still, both girls innocently asleep, their even breathing the only sound. So, smiling a little, Mother tiptoed down again.

THREE

The Club

JOAN'S club gave a welcome stimulant to the hot, drowsy vacation days which had long ago shed their luster and were gathering the dust of aimless boredom. Mother was delighted with the idea and promised help whenever necessary; but Joan said that the purpose of the club was to *give* help, not to *ask* for any, and she grandly waived all adult interference.

Tilly and Dickie had accepted membership with alacrity and the main problem now was to find a meeting place. The Mitchells' yard was infested by Timmy, to whom nothing was sacred. Then Joan remembered the playhouse in the White Elephant's yard. Nobody was using it in particular, and there was no reason why she shouldn't fix it up and make a clubhouse of it. So she went there with the others, and they all worked hard with pails, scrubbing brushes and paint, hanging muslin before the glassless windows and repairing the hinges of the door. Mother donated a card table and the rest of the furniture the children made out of orange crates.

The first meeting was held in great style, Joan presiding with a little hammer from a toy of Timmy's. He had lost the bench with pegs that belonged to it, and he only used it to terrorize his relatives, so it was mere justice to dedicate it to a nobler cause.

Those meetings were fun. The children gradually worked out a ritual. Peter stood sentry and asked for the password, which was different every time. When all the members had arrived and had entered the little house, they had to salute the flag and repeat the pledge of the club, which was to help their country in every way they could. Then they sang "Anchors Aweigh" for Daddy or "Into the wild blue yonder" for Uncle Jim, and Joan opened the business part of the meeting with a blow of her hammer on a breadboard, after which the various members had to show what they had done since the last meeting. Then Joan usually held a speech and the refreshments were served.

A paper pinned to the wall of the clubhouse showed the status of the club members in neatly typewritten words, done by Patsy on Mother's typewriter when she wasn't looking. It said:

FIVE FOR VICTORY CLUB
Members:

NAMES	RANKS		AGES
Joan Mitchell,	presedent	10 ½	years old
Patsy Mitchell,	sectatery	8	years old
Peter Mitchell,	treasuare	6	years old
Tilly Brewer		10	years old
Dicky Carter		6	years old
Angela Mitchell, mascot		3 ¾	years old
Timmy Mitchell, mascot		1 ¼	years old

Whenever a member had distinguished himself he got a star after his name. Patsy had a box of them, and she often counted to see how many there were, so they gradually changed from gold to brown. Joan got most of her stars collecting scrap. Peter was official bottle collector, keeping the pennies he got for them in a cardboard box. Every time there were ten he bought a stamp and pasted it in a book marked: "V for Victory bond." Another source of income was the victory garden, where Mother's beans were being devoured by beetles because she couldn't buy the spray which would have killed them. Peter picked them off the plants for her at the cheap rate of twenty for a penny, but there were so many that the treasury was doing very well indeed. Besides earning, Peter also saved. He saved soap. The results, at first, were rather unfortunate. Mother had to explain to him that it took much more soap to launder a lot of towels than to clean a pair of hands, before he would condescend to use soap again while washing. He was still careful never to wash any part of his body unless absolutely necessary. He usually climbed

up on the clothesbasket with his knee on the washbasin and examined what he could in the mirror to be sure he didn't clean too much by mistake. The effect was rather spotty and the saving went unnoticed, because Angela had a passion for washing her dolls and invariably left the soap to melt in the water; so Peter might just as well have used his share of it first. In fact, Mother accused him of making this war effort because he was scared of a little water, whereupon Peter smiled a wise smile and said nothing.

Patsy was the least active member of the club. She was the dreamer of the family and when you have your head full of fairies who get things done by magic it's hard to imagine yourself in a world at war where vulgar effort is required.

She did suggest, however, that a bomb shelter might be a good thing to have, in case of need. So the children dug a nice deep one in the White Elephant's yard, which they covered with planks and leaves. It was fun holding air-raid drills; Peter could imitate a siren remarkably well. But one day Angela discovered the shelter and sat down on it. The roof promptly caved in and she had to be rescued. The children never bothered to repair the shelter. They feared that if Angela fell through a bomb would too. And anyway, there were so many interesting things to do. They were busy all day long and Mother thought she had *never* known a more peaceful vacation.

One fine morning Joan was picking blackberries in the White Elephant's yard. She had discovered lots of them and they would be delicious for lunch, with honey and top milk. Peter and Patsy helped her, though they ate more than they picked. Tilly was cleaning the clubhouse and Dickie was busy making himself a bow and arrows. Birds twittered in the bushes, sprays of honeysuckle and masses of wild morning glories sweetened the air, attracting tiny hummingbirds with their haze of wings or bustling, half blind bumblebees, who seemed to be murmuring "beg pardon, beg pardon," all the time. The old trees, partly strangled with ivy, bent their branches with merciful gestures, as if inviting children to climb up, and threw welcome shadows over the tangled grass. Butterflies flashed about like winged flowers, and over it all patches of blue sky seemed to smile down like a fairy mother's eyes. Joan drew a deep breath.

"Isn't it *gorgeous?*" she sighed. "Even terribly rich children don't often have such a lovely place to play in!"

At that moment there was a noise as of a car stopping near by, followed by the slam of its door. Footsteps came tapping on the stone steps of the White Elephant's house. Joan gave a squeak of alarm and hid behind the bramble bush. The other children also crouched low.

"I guess someone is coming to buy the place," whispered Peter. "Wouldn't that be *dreadful?*" With bated breath the children peered through gaps in the bush. They saw a lady talking with a gentleman on the porch of the White Elephant. The gentleman was dangling some keys in his hand and presently he fitted one into the door of the house. It swung open. He let the lady enter first and then followed her. A big boy of about twelve, who had been kicking pebbles on the pathway with a bored air, now called out:

"I'll go and look at the yard, Mother, I don't want to see any more houses," and walked straight at the bramble bush, doubtless attracted by the sparkle of its berries.

"My goodness, he is coming here," cried Joan, her heart throbbing loudly.

"So what?" asked Peter. "I'm not scared of him." And scrambling up, he boldly faced the new arrival. The boy stood still and scowled at him.

"What are you doing here?" he asked. "This isn't your yard."

"It isn't yours either," said Peter, picking a blackberry and popping it into his mouth.

"It is too," said the boy. "My Mother is going to rent the house and those berries belong to us. Give me that basket."

"She hasn't rented it yet," cried Joan, getting up. "And she won't, I bet you. It costs a lot to keep up." But she held the basket behind her back for safety's sake.

"We have lots of money," the boy remarked, looking down his nose. "We can take any place we like. This isn't so hot, though; the yard is nothing but a dump of weeds."

"It is not!" cried Joan fiercely. "It's the prettiest place in the world." She felt her cheeks getting red and wished they wouldn't. The boy's cheeks looked cool and pale. He seemed to enjoy Joan's outburst. Folding his arms, he leant against a tree trunk and sent her a teasing glance.

"Too bad," he muttered, "for you'll have to keep out of it in the future. I don't let strange children run around my yard." He flicked some dust off his trousers with his long fingers and then he studied his nails. "Too bad," he muttered again, shaking his head.

The children looked at him in disgust. Joan had a sudden, wild longing to throw all her berries in his face. Luckily for her lunch, however, fate intervened. A voice from the house called:

"Henry! Henry!" and the boy, stretching himself, separated his long body from the tree trunk.

"Here, Mom!" The boy turned and gave one last look at the dazed party of children, whose joy he had so successfully quenched.

"Remember now," he added, with a malicious look from the corner of his eye, "this yard is *mine* and you're to stay out, or you'll have *me* to reckon with." And with a sound much like the growling of a dangerous dog, he ran off to the house, thinking to himself:

"My, didn't I scare 'em; that girl looked plain *silly*!" and feeling rather a hero.

He might not have been quite so satisfied if he had heard what the "silly" girl said as she watched him out of sight, her eyes narrowed in concentrated rage.

"He thinks he's wonderful," she muttered through her teeth. "But I guess if Peter had been bigger he'd have acted different. He's nothing but a bully. He doesn't look much of a fighter. I bet . . ." she calculated, flexing a plump arm, "I bet if it came to that, I could beat him."

"Oh, forget it," said Peter, whose cheerful nature never dealt with troubles until they were fast upon him. "His Mother won't take the house, you'll see. It's too big and dirty; no one ever wants it. We'll never see Henry again." And he shot an arrow out of Dickie's bow. But Joan felt uneasy.

"He is sure to make his mother take the house now, out of spite, so he can keep us away," she thought. "I shouldn't have shown how much I liked the place. I should have said it was an awful place full of . . . full of skunks. Yes, that's what I should have said. I bet he's scared of skunks, he looks so tidy with his hair all plastered down. Oh, why am I such a fool?" And poor Joan groaned with misery. Tilly and Patsy were inclined to agree with Peter.

"So many people have been looking at the house," they said. "You'll see, nothing will come of it." Joan was the only one who feared the worst.

"I feel it in my bones," she moaned. "That pipsqueak is going to get the place and lord it over our lovely hut, and it will all be *wasted* on him, just *wasted*. Oh why am I such an *idiot* . . . !" There was no good to be got out of Joan that day.

FOUR

Roomers

BUT something happened to make Joan forget her fears for her beloved "White Elephant." The children had known for some time that Mother was worried about money and now apparently a climax had arrived in her affairs, for she announced that she was going to take a lodger. It was either that or let Cora go, who had been with the Mitchells since Joan was a baby. Besides, it was a patriotic duty with the Capital so short of living space.

Mother had thought it all out carefully. The storage room on the third floor could be made into a very nice bedroom, just like that of the girls, with a bath right beside it. But it would have to be cleaned up of course. Joan immediately seized her opportunity.

"That's just the sort of thing our club is for, Mother!" she cried eagerly. "We'll help you. Peter and Dickie can move the trash and carry off what has to go to the salvage while Patsy, Tilly and I scrub and paint the room for you. I *love* painting!"

Mother sighed with relief.

"That *will* be a help," she said gratefully. "I was wondering how I'd get it done, with the vegetables in the garden all ready for canning, too!"

The next few days the children worked very hard, finishing the room in record time. It looked fresh and clean, with its newly painted apple-green walls, rosebud curtains, and odds and ends of furniture. A gay rug covered the floor and a few bright pictures decorated the walls.

"Even the President wouldn't mind living here," said Joan proudly, wiping a damp curl out of her eyes. The three girls had flung themselves on the lodger's soft bed, feeling as if they'd never want to move again. At that moment Angela poked her face around the door.

"Oh, it's pretty here!" she cried and she clapped her hands, dropping her favorite doll. It was an unusual doll, accustomed to serve both as friend and pocketbook, on account of having no top to its head, only a hole, into which Angela stuffed her treasures. Now a cooky rolled out and Angela hastily retrieved it, crunching it between her teeth.

"Poor Traincrack," she murmured with her mouth full, gathering the doll into her arms again. No one knew where she had got that name; the other children didn't like it, but Angela remained obdurate and now everyone

was used to it. Meanwhile the girls had noticed the cooky and had discovered that they were hungry.

"Where did you get it?" they asked.

"From Mother," said Angela, taking a second one out of Traincrack's skull. "She says come down and have some lemonade."

"Goodness! Why didn't you tell us?" The girls flew downstairs, forgetting their weariness.

Mother was sitting in the rocker on the porch and on a table in front of her stood tall glasses of iced lemonade, huge half-moon slices of pink watermelon and a dish of cookies. Peter and Dickie, perched on the porch railing, were already half through their share and even Grannie had joined the party, lying in the hammock. Joan plopped into a canvas chair with a sigh of pleasure, and the others sat down on the front steps.

"Boy! Is that good!" they sighed, letting the cool lemonade run down their throats and pushing their noses into the moist fragrance of the watermelon.

"Well, you deserved it," said Mother. "You've worked hard. How is the room getting on?"

The girls looked at one another and laughed.

"It's finished!" said Joan triumphantly. "We put the furniture in, too; all the things you showed us. It looks so pretty, doesn't it, Angela?"

"Uh-huh!" cried Angela with enthusiasm.

"Well, that *is* a surprise," said Mother. "I must go up to see it. You children have no idea how useful you've been!"

"What are you going to do now? Do you want us to paint a sign with 'Room for Rent,' and put it up in the yard?" offered Joan generously.

"No," chuckled Mother. "We'll place an advertisement. Let me see, what shall we put in?"

"The bath," advised Grannie. "Say: 'Third floor room, bath, in private residence.' You can have that at the minimum rate."

"*Are* we a private residence?" asked Peter, surprised. "Father is an officer!" Mother and Grannie laughed.

" 'Third floor room, bath, in officer's residence' *would* look better," Mother admitted. "It has a kind of patriotic flavor."

The morning the advertisement was in the paper the whole family leant over Mother's shoulder to admire it, except Timmy, who was too busy pouring oatmeal on his head.

"I bet everyone'll want to come and live in an *officer's* residence," remarked Peter proudly.

"We'll soon find out," said Mother.

There were quite a few phone calls that morning from

various people who wanted to see the room. The first visitor turned out to be a rather elegant lady, whose face was blurred by a dotted black veil. The children quickly hid behind the chairs and drapes of the living room. They had arranged to do this so people wouldn't be over-whelmed by all the children at once. Later, if the general outlook was favorable, the cleanest would come forward to shake hands. Mother hurriedly led the lady upstairs, trying to ignore a peculiar noise, like that of a dying hyena, which came from Peter's hiding place. The lady sighed audibly when she saw she had to mount a second flight of stairs.

"Third floor!" she said, frowning and pulling up her nose.

"It was in the advertisement," Mother reminded her patiently.

"Oh, was it? I can't remember. I've looked at so many of these places," said the lady, pronouncing "places" as if she meant "pigsties."

Mother proudly opened the door of the room on which the children had labored so hard. It still smelt of fresh paint and the sun slanted sheaves of light across the green walls causing the rosebuds on the curtains to glow. But the lady looked disappointed.

"Oh," she said. Then she turned to inspect the bath-room. "Hm. Well . . ." she thought for a moment and her face behind the veil seemed rather glum. "It isn't what I had *hoped*, but . . ." suddenly her well-bred voice changed its pitch as she shrieked "Ouch!" and jumped a foot high. It was only Angela who had trudged upstairs and now at-tempted to brush past the lady's nylon stockings. The lady grabbed her skirt and shook it, as if she expected a second Angela to drop from its folds.

"Children?" she squeaked, her nose turning up so much that Mother was afraid it would never come down again. "Why didn't you tell me you had *children?* This wouldn't suit me *at all!*" and she ran downstairs as fast as she could without losing her high-heeled pumps. Angela watched her leave the house and noted with interest that the lady said neither "good-by" nor "thank you." So, peering around the door which the lady had left open, she shouted:

"Good-by, lady, good-by I said!" and closed the door securely, giving it a few extra pushes. Meanwhile the other children had crawled out of their hiding places.

"Good thing she didn't stay, Mother," said Joan. "I'd be scared to have her in the house, she is too elegant."

"Yes," agreed Mother. "I never knew I could be so happy about *not* renting a room," and she did a little dance with the children. But the day was young yet and Mother remembered her duties.

"You watch at the window and warn me if more callers come," she told Joan. "I want to talk to Cora."

Cora was washing the breakfast dishes in the kitchen. She was a much more sensible person than Mother. She had had a hard life and knew what to expect of people. Mother valued her opinion a lot. Now Mother was telling her about the lady with the turned-up nose and Cora was giggling over the soap-suds.

"If that lady had wanted to stay," Mother asked helplessly, "what *could* I have done? How does one get rid of people one doesn't like? Does one say: 'Oh no, lady, you're too snooty?' "

Cora laughed so, she almost dropped a plate. "No, ma'am," she said. "You just raise the price."

"Oh." Mother went thoughtfully back to the living room. This lady would have been at least a hundred dollars a month, she decided. Rather like a reverse kind of report, the lower the better. Meanwhile the children were dancing in front of the window.

"There's another one, Mother!" cried Joan. "He is a man and he looks nice. Do we have to hide, Mother? Do we? He doesn't look as if he'd be scared!"

"No, no! You can stay," said Mother hurriedly. The sooner people found out she had children the better, she thought; it saved steps.

Mother had to show the room to many more visitors, before a lady finally decided to take it. By that time most of the children had lost interest and had gone outside to play. They were told about it at lunch.

"She is a Miss Merryvale, a schoolteacher," said Mother.

"And she'll be very good for us," announced Grannie,

putting some margarine on her bread. "She'll make us sit up."

"Sit up?" asked Patsy, looking around.

"Like a dog doing tricks," Joan explained.

"I wish we *had* a dog."

"You know Daddy doesn't like them," Mother reminded her.

"Why doesn't Daddy like dogs?" asked Patsy.

"Oh, don't you know? Because of the fleas," said Peter.

Joan knew, all right. A few years ago the Mitchells had gone to the seaside for a vacation, subletting their house to a man with a dog. When they came back after Labor Day, Daddy had spent his evenings picking fleas off his socks and drowning them in a glass of water. He seemed so interested in catching them, wearing white socks for the purpose, that Joan couldn't understand why he made such a fuss. But the end was that the whole family had to go for a walk while some men put the fleas to sleep.

After that, whenever you said "dog," Daddy would jump as if you'd pinched him.

"Miss Cherrydale seems a pleasant person," Grannie observed, ignoring Joan's interruption about dogs.

"Merryvale," Mother corrected her, but Grannie was terrible about names. She'd be sure to forget.

"We shall all have to be very careful about our manners," Mother went on, and she spent the rest of the meal telling the children what not to do when Miss Merryvale had come, until the children wondered whether there'd be *any* fun left in the world at all.

FIVE

Miss Merryvale Arrives

THE day Miss Merryvale was expected Grannie was invited out to dine with friends.

"It's just as well, my dear," Grannie told Mother as she was putting on her hat in front of the hall mirror. "That poor Miss Berrypail will have enough people to get acquainted with the first day."

"Merryvale," Mother corrected, but Grannie didn't pay any attention.

At her age you didn't have to bother with names any more, she thought. People excused everything in an old person. Perhaps it wasn't quite fair of Grannie to take advantage of that, at least that's what Mother said, but

Grannie cried, "Pish, tosh," and flounced off in her finery, which made her look very elegant and not a bit like Grannie.

The three oldest grandchildren accompanied her a part of the way, patting her silk coat with admiring hands, telling her to save them some candy and crying "Good-by! Good-by!" for a long time after she was out of sight. Then their attention was arrested by a big moving van which rumbled past them and stopped in front of the "White Elephant."

The children watched it with alarm. It was two weeks now since Henry had first threatened to oust them from their paradise, and when nothing had happened in the meantime the children had begun to hope that Henry's mother wasn't going to rent the house after all. Now the moving van confirmed Joan's worst predictions. The children saw several men carry furniture from the van into the White Elephant house, and their eyes filled with tears.

"I can't *bear* it," muttered Joan. "It isn't *fair* that Henry should have it all!" and she clenched her fists.

"What will happen to our club now?" asked Peter. "I'm sure Henry won't let us use the playhouse." Joan looked startled. She hadn't thought of that yet.

"And all our things are in it," she cried. "The flag we bought with our own money and our war bond book and *everything!* If Henry finds them he'll keep them, I know that much! Come along, we'll have to rescue them right away before he comes. Don't let the moving men see you; they may think we are robbers or something."

Cautiously the children crept around the White Elephant's yard until trees hid them from the house. Then they wormed themselves through a gap in the hedge and ran swiftly to the clubhouse. Luckily nothing had been touched there; all was as they had left it. Apparently Henry was not yet around.

It took several trips before the children had carried all their belongings home, dumping them in the garage for the time being.

"Goodness knows *where* we'll hold our meetings now," Joan grumbled bitterly. Before she went on the last trip she took one long look at her beloved paradise. Embracing the card table, which was loaded with other possessions, she mournfully took leave of the trailing branches, waving grass plumes and tangled shrubbery. Tears dripped down her nose and splashed on the table. At last she wrenched herself away from the beautiful spectacle and followed the other children through the gap in the hedge. As she was hurrying down the sidewalk with her load, her eyes still misted with tears, she suddenly banged into someone and dropped the card table with all its superimposed objects. They rolled and clattered on the pavement, but Joan had to brush the tears out of her eyes before she could see what had happened.

A small and dignified lady had apparently lost her balance and was sitting on the sidewalk, too, surrounded by the contents of a suitcase, which had burst open from the shock.

"Oh, I'm so sorry, did I run into you?" asked Joan, blushing furiously. She hoped the lady hadn't seen her tears.

As a matter of fact, the lady was feeling much too uncomfortable to notice anything. "Yes, you did," she said, a note of irritation in her voice. "And now look at all my things! Why don't you watch where you are going?"

Joan knew she ought to explain, but she didn't know where to start, so she kept staring stupidly at the flustered

lady who kept sitting on the sidewalk, glaring back at her. Luckily they were rescued out of their predicament by Peter and Patsy, who had turned back upon hearing the commotion. Now they immediately offered to help the lady. They seemed to recognize her.

"Oh, Miss Merryvale," cried Patsy, "what happened to you? Shall I help you up? Oh goodness, you're all dusty at the back; wait, I'll brush you off. Peter, you put the clothes back in the suitcase; don't wrinkle them. Come along, this is our house. I suppose you were going to our house?" And Patsy took Miss Merryvale by the hand, leading her up the front steps. "Isn't it funny, us bumping into you like this? Peter has your suitcase, it'll be all right.

Peter is very careful. He always lays the table for Mother and he only once broke a dish."

Joan had picked up the card table and the other things and now followed Miss Merryvale and Patsy. She listened with admiration to Patsy's eloquence. Patsy was sometimes timid at games, but when it came to strangers there was no one like her. You'd think there wasn't anything to be scared of, the way she acted.

"I hope you'll like staying with us," Patsy continued, giving Miss Merryvale's hand a little squeeze. "We'll like it, I know."

Miss Merryvale had now been soothed completely. In fact, she was charmed. "I'm sure I shall, too," she told Patsy kindly.

They had arrived at the house now and Mother came out of the kitchen to greet the guest. It was Cora's day off.

"How do you do, Miss Merryvale," she said. "Children, you show Miss Merryvale her room. The food will be ready in a minute." And she hurried back to the stove.

When the children had accomplished their mission and returned with Miss Merryvale, dinner was served, consisting of a large dish of steaming spaghetti, covered with a thick tomato sauce and surrounded by savory meatballs. But just as they made ready to sit down to it, Angela and Timmy wandered in from the yard, looking so muddy that Mother had to wash them.

"You start dinner," she called out to Joan. "Don't let it get cold!"

"Yes, Mother!" said Joan. "Please sit down, Miss Merryvale." And pink with importance she began to serve the spaghetti, holding her breath for fear she would mess on the clean tablecloth.

Meanwhile, Patsy felt it was her duty to keep up the

conversation. "Do you like fairy tales?" she asked, when Miss Merryvale had started on her spaghetti, curling it up daintily around her fork.

"Oh yes," said Miss Merryvale. "When I was a little girl I loved fairy tales. Of course, I haven't read any now for a long time, but I remember how wonderful they are, full of fairies and princesses."

"Do you have Royal Blood?" asked Patsy.

"No, I don't," said Miss Merryvale, startled.

"I don't either," admitted Patsy wistfully. "Don't you wish you had though?"

"Not at all. I'm a republican," Miss Merryvale retorted.

"But wouldn't it be much nicer to be a princess and marry a prince?" urged Patsy. Miss Merryvale didn't answer. She was too busy curling up a long string of spaghetti until it was small enough to eat.

"Which fairy tale do you like best?" continued Patsy.

Miss Merryvale wiped her mouth with her napkin, though it wasn't at all dirty, took a sip of water, holding her little finger gracefully in the air, and said:

"Let me see. Isn't there one called 'The Sleeping Beauty'? Oh, and 'Little Red Ridinghood.' We mustn't forget 'Little Red Ridinghood.'"

"They're *eas*y," remarked Peter scornfully, taking a big helping of meatballs. "I like 'Jack the Giant Killer' best. I bet Hitler couldn't do much against *him*. Hitler isn't as good, even, as the *giant*."

"Aren't you glad *we* aren't giants?" asked Patsy. "Because giants always kill people who sleep in their house. They say:

> Though you may lodge with me tonight,
> You shall not see the morning light."

"Yes," cried Peter, "or they say:

> Be he living or be he dead,
> His heart this night shall kitchen my bread.

That means that he'd put it on his bread with pepper and salt on it," ended Peter, grinning happily.

"For goodness' sake," said Miss Merryvale, putting down her fork.

"Yes, but Jack knew what to do with giants, didn't he, Peter?" cried Patsy. "He put hasty pudding in a bag and hid it under his clothes and then he cut it open so the hasty pudding ran out as hasty as anything."

"Yes, and the giant said, 'Odds splutter hur nails hur can do so hurself,' and ripped open his belly with his knife so all the insides came out!" shrieked Peter, shaking with laughter.

"And the other giant was so mad he cried, 'Then I shall tear thee with my teeth, suck thy blood and grind thy bones to powder,' " Joan added with a chuckle.

"I bet Hitler couldn't beat that," Peter crowed triumphantly.

When Mother came back, carrying sleepy Timmy and holding a clean and subdued Angela by the hand, she noticed that Miss Merryvale looked a trifle pale.

"I hope the dinner is all right?" she asked anxiously.

"Oh, it's quite all right," Miss Merryvale assured her politely. "But do you think fairy tales are suitable for children?"

Mother put Timmy in his highchair and tied his bib. "Why yes," she said surprised. And she looked at her children, who were eating very nicely with clean faces and clean hands, not a speck messed on the tablecloth.

Mother felt proud of them. What a good impression they must be making.

"Of course they can read fairy tales," she purred. "Wouldn't you like some more spaghetti, Miss Merryvale?"

"No, thank you," said Miss Merryvale.

Miss Merryvale was fond of children. She was a kind teacher and her classes were always orderly. But she had been an only child herself and she hadn't seen much of children outside school. It would be very interesting, she decided, to live with the Mitchells.

All the same she was rather disagreeably surprised when she was awakened suddenly the next morning by a loud, crashing noise.

"What can that be?" she cried, grabbing her bathrobe and running into the girls' room. "What's happened?"

Joan woke up with a start. "It's nothing," she murmured sleepily. "Only Timmy, shaking his crib."

"Good gracious!" muttered Miss Merryvale. "At six o'clock in the morning!" And she hurried back to bed. But every time she fell into the soft mood which comes just before sleep, Timmy gave an especially ferocious shake to his iron crib, rocking the foundations of the house and jerking her back into consciousness.

"Good Heavens, does he never *stop?*" she sighed. "Why don't they *discipline* the boy? I must lend Mrs. Mitchell my book on child training. This is preposterous." Feeling thoroughly annoyed, Miss Merryvale got out of bed and put on her stockings. It was just as well she did, for now the household was waking in earnest.

Several doors slammed at once, causing a picture, which had been clinging for dear life to a wobbly nail, to drop down with a bang. There were shrieks from Angela, who wasn't being let in somewhere. Then a call from Mother.

"Joan and Patsy, it's time to get up!" Joan's voice answered, "Yes, Mother, I'm up, but I can't wake Patsy."

Sounds of a scuffle in the girls' room, and a flying pillow collided with Miss Merryvale as she left the bathroom, hitting the toothbrush out of her hand.

"Ouch!" she squealed, "can't one even dress in peace in this house?"

But a strong smell of fried eggs and coffee consoled her. She found her way to the dining room where Mother greeted her pleasantly.

"Good morning, Miss Merryvale. Would you like some oatmeal?"

"Yes, please," said Miss Merryvale, noticing that she was hungry. She hadn't eaten much the night before.

"Let me pour you some coffee," continued Mother. "What are your plans for today? Your school hasn't started yet, has it?"

"No, but I have some work to do at the library today," said Miss Merryvale, feeling her good humor coming back again. The room was beautifully still. Timmy sat in his highchair, pink with soap and water. Peter, also washed, with a clean shirt on, was silenced by an enormous plateful of oatmeal and honey. Grannie came down and made a cheerful remark about the weather. She handed Miss Merryvale the paper and Miss Merryvale saw at a glance that we hadn't lost the war yet. The cuckoo clock cleared its throat and announced leisurely that it was eight o'clock. Miss Merryvale felt it was a privilege to live in a real home. But suddenly the peace was shattered by Angela, who came whirling into the dining room, curls flying,

a shoe on one foot, a slipper on the other. She had her
arms full of dolls but clamored for more.

"Where's Markie?" she cried. "Where *is* Markie? I've
lost Markie!" and let out a wail that seemed to slide like a
knife down Miss Merryvale's backbone, cutting her in
two. At the same moment the older girls entered with hair
cascading down like the tangled manes of wild horses, and
wanted to have it "done." Timmy looked up, saw life was
becoming interesting, whooped, and threw his toast across
the table, right into Miss Merryvale's cup, upsetting it. As
Miss Merryvale tried to stop the stream of coffee before it
reached her new skirt, she felt something touch her ankle
and jumped up with a yell. It wasn't an animal, though;
only Angela, who was crawling on the floor in search of
Markie. But Miss Merryvale thought she had had enough.
Murmuring that she wasn't hungry, she left her egg un-
touched, snatched her hat and rushed out of the house.

Meanwhile things had quieted down in the dining room as quickly as they had boiled up.

"If Miss Merryvale had only waited a *minute*," complained Mother. "I had a new cup of coffee poured for her and now there is an egg going to waste at fifty cents a dozen."

"Oh no, it isn't," said Joan. "Give it to me."

"But you had one already," protested Mother.

"I could eat ten," Joan assured her. Mother slid the egg on her plate.

"There's one thing I know, though," she said grimly. "You and Patsy are going to be bobbed and banged. I've got enough to fuss over in the mornings."

"Oh, Mother!" Patsy's eyes filled with tears. "Please don't! We'll be good!" Mother looked at her in surprise.

"It isn't a punishment . . ." she began.

"What do you think Mother means?" giggled Joan.

Patsy's eyes looked large and scared. "It sounds *awful*," she sighed.

"It only means Mother's going to cut our hair," explained Joan. "Boy! Won't it feel good!" Patsy smiled with relief. Then she looked worried again.

"Angela's too?" she asked. They all looked at Angela, who sat sweetly between her dolls, feeding Markie, who had been rescued from under the piano. With eyes like melted sky and locks like solid sunshine, she looked as if she could never do a naughty thing in her life.

"No," said Mother. "We'll leave Angela her curls. For if we take those away, what's left?"

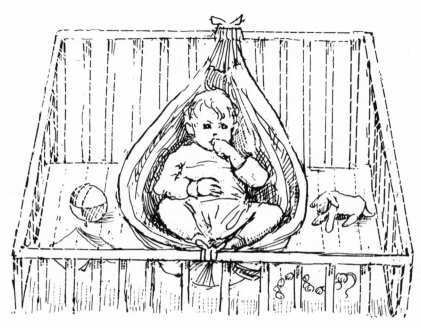

SIX

Miss Merryvale Leaves

AFTER a while Miss Merryvale got a little more used to the Mitchells. She learned to step over gates, dodge airplanes, and look out for scattered toys, but she never got reconciled to Timmy. Timmy was a great disappointment to her. She had always thought of babies as pink, cuddly things with innocent, blue eyes as they are depicted on magazine covers. Timmy shattered this illusion. Far from being pink and cuddly, he was seldom clean, unless just after a bath, and always averse to any form of affection. Besides, he had a cold of which he took no notice whatever, only objecting strenuously when a charitable person tried to blow his nose. He had an enormous appetite and left traces of every meal on his suits and bibs, if not in his hair. And he was happiest when he could pull some valuable bit of furniture to pieces. He reminded Miss Merryvale irresistibly of an animal at the zoo, especially when he stared at her between the bars of his play-pen or swung lazily in the little hammock his mother had strung up inside it.

But Angela was a sweet little thing. Miss Merryvale had taken a liking to her from the beginning and one after-noon, when she had nothing else to do, she invited the child up to her room. Angela was delighted.

"Now?" she cried, skipping up and down. "Right now?" And without waiting she ran upstairs on hands and feet, showing the patched seat of a pair of brief pants.

"Wait till I bring my babies!" she cried, running into her bedroom and emerging with an armful. Poor Train-crack dragged over the floor, causing Angela to trip and fall on her nose. Miss Merryvale had to sit on the stairs and comfort her, and she had to kiss Traincrack, too.

"Because she is hurt more; I fell on her." And then she had to kiss all the other dolls, and Traincrack wanted to ride piggyback. Miss Merryvale was to be the pig and hop about on all fours, saying "Guggug!" in pig language. Angela assured her that Grannie always did it and Mom-mie always did it and Daddy always did it, and when Miss Merryvale said firmly that she *refused* to do it, Angela began to cry again. Miss Merryvale hastily found a forgot-ten chocolate in her bag which coaxed away Angela's tears once more.

"Now come along to my room and I'll tell you a story," Miss Merryvale urged. She knew a sweet story about a little girl, just like Angela, whom *everybody* loved; but Angela looked worried. She didn't seem to have her

Teddy bear; she *believed* it was downstairs. Miss Merryvale would have to wait while she went to fetch him. It took quite a while before Angela returned with a jam sandwich instead of a Teddy bear, but the Teddy bear was finally found under Mother's bed and pressed against the sandwich, so that Angela had to lick him and the bread in turn to get all the jam. At last Miss Merryvale succeeded in getting Angela to the third floor, but by this time the child looked rather sticky, with a blackberry tip to her nose and her hands full of chocolate and jam.

"You'd better come to the bathroom first," declared Miss Merryvale. "Then we'll wash those little paws." Angela consented on condition that Teddy bear would be washed too, and with the pink soap, not the white. It smelt so lovely. Miss Merryvale had to smell it too. She might have smelt it before, but this was the first time she could smell it together with Angela. And there was to be a lot of soapsuds. And Miss Merryvale was not to help her. All she had to do was to sit on the clothesbasket and have wet hands pushed into her face to see "how clean." Angela could do it all perfectly well herself; in fact, she was not to be torn away. It became a long argument and a tussle of wills and a promise of a piece of candy . . . no *five*, *and* some cookies, before Angela agreed to place her wet, sudsy hands in the bath towel and be dried. The bathroom looked as if ten people had laundered their clothes in it, and Miss Merryvale suddenly noticed that she had a headache. She was, therefore, not quite so kind and cheerful as she led Angela into her room. Angela immediately demanded her wages of candy and cookies, undoing all the good of the washing in a few seconds.

Miss Merryvale sighed.

"Now come and sit in my lap and I'll tell you a lovely

little story about a little girl *just* like you," she began in a bright, brittle tone of voice.

"What's that?" asked Angela, poking at a book.

"That's a dictionary, dear. Now just sit in my lap . . ."

"And what's *that?* " asked Angela, running to a picture and feeling it with sticky fingers.

"Don't touch, honey. That's a photograph. Come and sit on my lap now, and I'll tell you the story . . ."

"And what's this?" asked Angela, lifting a statue from the chest of drawers.

"Oh be careful, darling. That's an angel."

"An *angel?* " chanted Angela rapturously, and with a whoop she threw the little figure up in the air. Before Miss Merryvale's horrified eyes it went smash on the floor, both wings broken. Miss Merryvale gathered up the pieces,

trying to fit them together. There was a mist over her eyes. The little angel was very dear to her.

"Why did you do that?" she asked in a choked voice. Angela stood still and solemn, much impressed by what had happened.

"Why *did* you?" Miss Merryvale repeated, sternness creeping into her voice.

But Angela wouldn't answer. Her eyes were like deep blue wells of mystery. Miss Merryvale gently put the broken angel back on the chest of drawers. Then she took Angela's dolls and flung them into the passage. Then she took Angela and pushed her out after them. Then she locked the door. She stood for a moment, thinking. And then she threw the book on child training into the wastepaper basket.

Meanwhile Angela walked soberly downstairs, trailing Traincrack. Of all the dolls only Traincrack shared Angela's misfortunes. Mother was in the living room writing a letter to Daddy. Ordinarily, Angela would know better than to disturb her, but this time she had made a stupendous discovery and it *had* to be shared.

"Mother," she began.

"Yes, dear," said Mother in an abstracted way, going on writing. But Angela wanted Mother's undivided attention.

"Mother," she repeated several times, with increasing vigor. At last Mother's pen stopped, her eyes wandered from her letter and met Angela's.

"Oh, it's *you*," she said.

"Yes, Mother." Angela's little heart-shaped face looked pale, her eyes round and troubled.

"Well, what is it?" asked Mother, putting down her pen and leaning back in her chair with an encouraging smile.

"You said . . . you said . . . you said angels could fly . . ." stammered Angela.

"So they can," said Mother.

"No, they can't." Angela's eyes were reproachful. "I tried and now Mary-veil is angry."

It was some time before Mother got the whole story and could come to the rescue with a pot of glue, mending the angel so well you'd never think it had been broken and explaining to Angela the difference between spirit angels and china ones.

But that was not the end of Miss Merryvale's troubles. Joan, Patsy, and Peter had finally found a meeting place for their club in Tilly's cellar. It was rather a damp cellar and after a few meetings Joan began to sneeze. It didn't take long before all the other little Mitchells were sneezing, too. Mother ordered them to bed and soon the house was filled with the songs of steaming kettles and the smells of camphorated oil, licorice and turpentine.

Miss Merryvale lived in fear and trembling. If there was anything she dreaded, it was germs. And the house simply *teemed* with them. As she crept cautiously upstairs, a handkerchief pressed against her nose, some child would be sure to cough the minute she passed the open door of its room. With a squeal Miss Merryvale would rush on to the third floor, only to find it strewn with used paper handkerchiefs.

"Oh, Biss Berryvale," Joan and Patsy would cry eagerly. "Cob ad visit us; we have't seed adybody today!"

"No, no," Miss Merryvale would answer hurriedly, escaping into her room and locking the door. There she'd gargle, put drops in her nose, take a lozenge in her mouth, and sit down to wait for a cold. To her surprise she continued in excellent health. But she took care to spend most of her time at the library.

Mother had her hands full trying to keep the three oldest patients quiet. At last she remembered a doctor's toy set which she had put aside in a drawer for emergencies. It was a large set, containing the usual paper spectacles, printed cards, pills, wooden thermometer and toy stethoscope. The children hailed it with joy and were soon playing a grand game of showing tongues and feeling pulses and lying for dead under a sheet. Mother then went to look how the little ones were getting on and found that they had provided their own amusement by pulling all the feathers from their pillows. Looking at the snowy mass on the floor it seemed strange that it had all once fitted into two little pillows. Mother was so busy clearing up the mess that she didn't hear Miss Merryvale come home. Mounting the staircase in her usual swift, silent fashion, Miss Merryvale tried to dodge the germs that were lying in wait for her. But scarcely had she reached the top floor when she stood petrified. The door of the girls' room was severely closed, a most unusual thing in itself, and on it hung a card, which Miss Merryvale studied.

Then a strange spirit seemed to take possession of her. She rushed into her room, hauled forth her trunk and suitcase, and flung all her possessions into them, higgledy piggledy, even dumping her precious angel against her bedroom slippers. Having firmly closed both receptacles, she took up her suitcase and tiptoed downstairs with it, holding her breath. After reaching the front door in safety, she was out of the house in one leap, slamming the door behind her and descending the steps like a Messerschmitt with a Spitfire on its tail.

Mother heard the door slam and went to the hall. "Is it you, Miss Merryvale?" she asked, wanting to tell her that the children were much better and that the doctor had said they could get up tomorrow. But when there was no answer, she thought it must have been the screen door she heard slamming in the wind. Mother didn't think of Miss Merryvale again until the telephone rang just before dinner.

"Yes?" Mother said, lifting the receiver to her ear. She was surprised to hear it was Miss Merryvale.

"I'm speaking from the Wardman Park Hotel," Miss Merryvale said. "I haven't had it and I don't want to be quarantined with school starting next week. It may last for months, with five children. I'm terribly sorry but I just packed and went. The Express will call for my trunk. I hope you don't mind."

"No indeed," Mother murmured soothingly. "It's quite

all right. Don't worry." Then she put down the receiver and looked blank. "Maybe she is sick, or something," she thought. "Whatever *could* she be talking about? I'd better go up to her room." Mother went upstairs and glanced at the trunk standing forlornly in Miss Merryvale's dismantled room. Then she noticed the card hanging on the door of the girls' room.

"Scarlet Fever" it said in big red letters. Mother leaned against the doorpost and laughed until the tears came into her eyes. The children opened the door and wanted to know what was so funny. Grannie came up from the second floor and wanted to hear, too. So they all sat down on Joan's bed and Mother told the story. Soon the others were laughing as heartily as Mother.

"It was in our doctor's set," Peter explained unnecessarily.

"But we'd better tell her. . . ." began Joan.

"No, no," said Grannie. "That would only make her feel foolish."

"Besides," said Mother, "it would be unkind. She has gone to a lot of expense getting a room at the Wardman Park Hotel and she may as well think it's for a good reason. She wasn't happy here anyway."

"No, it's all for the best," Grannie agreed placidly.

The next day Grannie first saw the advertisement in the paper and showed it to the family.

"Wanted: a quiet room," it said, "by elderly schoolteacher in orderly household with few or no children."

"That's Miss Flurrytail, of course," said Grannie. "Well, I hope she finds it. She was a nice lady and we led her a hard life." Nobody seemed sad about it, though. Only Mother sighed as she remarked, "And now we have to find another roomer."

SEVEN

The First Pet

JOAN swung in the hammock on the front porch. For a
wonder nobody else wanted it. Mother had taken
Timmy out shopping, Angela was helping Cora bake a
pie, Peter was playing "kick the can" with some boys in
the alley, and Patsy was in Grannie's room, crying because her hair had been cut. It looked very nice on her,
but Patsy said no princess in any fairy tale ever had short
hair, and Grannie was trying to console her.

So Joan could swing in peace, how blessed that was!
Usually you could only hang on for a couple of seconds
among a crowd clamoring "I wanna swing! I wanna
swing!" until somebody forcibly pushed you off. Not that

Joan disliked having brothers and sisters; she was very proud of them. She often discussed them with her friend the traffic policeman, whom you must not call "cop"; that wasn't polite.

"Mother has an awful time with us all," she had confided to him once. "But she likes it. I'm going to be a mother too when I grow up, because all my forefathers have been mothers."

The policeman had looked surprised and afterward Joan realized that half of them probably had been fathers. But at any rate, Joan planned to have a large family. She was already thinking of what she would do to educate them properly. She didn't quite approve of Mother's method. Mother was too lenient. The minute Peter or Angela soft-soaped her she gave in to them and then, of course, she had more trouble next time. Joan wasn't going to make that mistake. With twelve children you can't afford to. She had found an interesting book in Miss Merryvale's wastebasket about how to train a child. Joan meant to read the book so she could help Mother train Angela, but she'd have to do it in her free time, for school was starting again tomorrow. Joan wasn't as sorry as she would have been two weeks ago, before the White Elephant was barred to her. Vacation had become rather tedious since then. The club had languished for want of a proper meeting place; Mother had forbidden further gatherings in Tilly's cellar. Once they had met in Miss Merryvale's empty room, but now Mr. Spencer had come to live with them that was no longer possible.

Mr. Spencer was a very nice man, thought Joan. Everyone liked him, even Grannie. Of course, he was more or less Grannie's age and shared many of her ideas. Mr. Spencer was English, but he knew a lot about Holland.

He and Grannie were always talking of those far-off countries and the children loved to listen to them. Mr. Spencer had told Grannie a very sad tale about Rotterdam. Mr. Spencer's daughter, Irene, and his little granddaughter, Eunice, had been visiting Rotterdam when the Germans invaded Holland. Mr. Randall, Eunice's father, had to do some business there, and he had taken his family along for the trip. In those days Holland was a peaceful spot where you could eat better than anywhere in Europe. Nobody thought that Hitler would invade Holland just after he had signed a paper promising to respect her neutrality. But he did, and when the news came Mr. Spencer had felt terribly worried and had telegraphed and telegraphed to his daughter but there had been no answer. Everything was in such confusion in those days, Mr. Spencer doubted whether the telegrams ever arrived. Then Rotterdam was bombed, and the last Mr. Spencer had heard of his daughter, granddaughter, and son-in-law was that they had been in the most heavily bombed part of the city and were presumed to be dead. As Mr. Spencer had never heard from them again, he feared they must be. He knew that if they had been alive they would somehow, in these three years, have contrived to get through a message to relieve his anxiety.

Mother said she felt sorry for Mr. Spencer. A child was always your child, no matter how grown up, and to lose one was agony. You could see that Mr. Spencer still felt sad about it, though he had two other children, a son in the Navy and another son in a training camp for flyers. Not that Mr. Spencer was a gloomy person. Oh no, he was always cheerful and kind and polite about saying "Good morning," and "Thank you, my dear," and "Please, would you mind?" even to Angela. It had made Angela quite polite herself. She now also began the day by saying "Good morning!" to everybody.

Angela was funny, thought Joan. When she had first seen Mr. Spencer sitting with Mother and Grannie in the living room, she had asked in a loud whisper, "Who is the one that isn't Us?"

Mr. Spencer had heard and had immediately introduced himself in proper style. You could see he knew a lot about children. He and Angela were great friends. Only the other day Angela had pushed a prickleburr into the palm of Mr. Spencer's hand.

"That's for the Germans," she told him, "to put in their hair. It won't come out." She had heard that Mr. Spencer was working to get ammunition and equipment for the English soldiers, and a prickleburr was the most powerful weapon she could think of. Mr. Spencer had understood right away. He had gravely put the prickleburr in an envelope and had addressed it:

"To Mr. Hitler, with the compliments of Angela."

Joan smiled as she worked with one toe to swing herself higher and higher. From the street below came a squeaking sound. That was Mother, with Timmy in his buggy. You couldn't see much of Timmy on account of the groceries piled around him. Just the top of his head stuck out. Joan noticed he was eating something. Cookies, probably, to make him sit still or the eggs would drop.

"Help me," cried Mother from below. "You take Timmy and I'll take the groceries."

"All right," said Joan, sliding from the hammock and running down the steps.

"Come here, Angel, come here, my pet, come to Joanie. That's right, climb up. . . . Joan'll help you. Come then, honey, Joan'll lift you into your yard. There you are!"

"Look and see if there is glass anywhere," warned Mother, who staggered under a load of oranges, flour and sugar.

Joan stepped over the fence and wandered around the yard, looking about for sharp objects. Suddenly she jumped forward and knelt beside something which moved feebly in the grass. At first she thought it was a rat, but it didn't run away and its eyes, instead of being mean, were soft and dewy. Then she saw that it must be a baby squirrel. Its tail was thin and not bushy, but perhaps baby squirrels are like that, she thought. It was gray, like a mouse, and had tiny ears. It looked small and helpless, and didn't run away when Joan stretched out her hand to it.

"Oh, I'm glad Timmy didn't find it," she murmured, picking it up and holding it in the hollow of her palms. "If I had been lazy and hadn't done what Mother asked me, Timmy would surely have killed it. Yes, you may look, Timmy, but don't touch. It's a little squirrel, you see, a tiny one. I bet it's hungry, too. I must show Mother." She

walked back slowly and carefully, sheltering her treasure in cupped hands.

Mother was in the kitchen, putting away the groceries. She came when Joan called to her.

"Look what I found!"

Presently the whole family, Cora included, was gathered around the little foundling.

"You'll have to get a cage for it," Cora said.

"Try an apple basket," suggested Mother. She went with Joan to the basement and there they found several almost new bushelbaskets, lid and all. They chose the firmest and Mother folded an old blanket inside.

"That will make a nice cage," she said. The little squirrel seemed happy in his new home and didn't even try to climb the walls.

"He is very tiny," said Mother. "You'd better phone the zoo, Joan, to find out what we must do for him." Joan looked up the number in the telephone book and asked for "a person who knows about squirrels."

She got a Mr. Hollis, who seemed very interested. Joan realized that he must love animals almost as much as she, the way he spoke. He said he'd like to see the squirrel, and when Joan told him where she lived, he said he passed that way going home and would stop by. He could advise better when he had seen the baby. Joan felt very important as she put down the receiver. It was almost like being a mother and asking a doctor to come and see your sick child.

Meanwhile, other children in the neighborhood had heard of Joan's find and had come to see it. Quite a lot of them had gathered around the bushelbasket in the living room, but Joan wouldn't let them handle the squirrel.

"Mr. Hollis says not to touch him," she said, and stood sentinel. All they could do was to peer through the holes.

"I may keep him, Mother, mayn't I?" begged Joan, who already felt a mysterious bond between herself and the helpless little creature.

"Of course, you may keep him," said Mother. "If he lives; he does seem very young."

"Oh, dear God, let him live," prayed Joan silently and fervently.

Presently Mr. Hollis rang the doorbell. He was a kind young man with a grave face. When Joan had opened the basket for him, he took the little squirrel in his hands.

"It's strange . . ." he remarked. "It's too late in the year for a squirrel to be born. I guess he is a kind of freak and his mother abandoned him because he couldn't live through the winter."

"Oh, will he die?" asked Joan, her heart in her eyes.

Mr. Hollis looked at her and a flash of sympathy

seemed to pass between them. "*You* can take care of him," Mr. Hollis assured her. "But you have to nurse him like a baby, understand? And he has to sleep outside. Don't bring him into the house. As soon as you do that he'll get sick when he goes outside again. You'd have to keep him indoors always and that is no life for a squirrel. If you want him to be happy you *must* keep him in the fresh air."

"I understand," said Joan.

"I believe you do." And the young man glanced at her with an approving smile. "Take care *they* don't hurt him," he added, waving an accusing hand at the other children.

"Yes, I will," promised Joan.

"I shall now write you a formula to feed him," Mr. Hollis said solemnly. He took out his fountain pen and wrote on a pad of paper. Then he tore the top sheet off and gave it to Joan.

"He'll have to be fed every two hours with a medicine dropper," he said. "Keep him quiet and warm, in the open air, and clean his bed every day. If you have any trouble, just phone me." And bowing politely to the grown-ups and Joan, but ignoring the other children, he left. Mother took the paper out of Joan's hand and chuckled.

"I don't know what the world is coming to," she said. "Who could be bothered putting up a formula like that for a squirrel?"

"I'll do it, Mother," offered Joan.

"You'll do no such thing," Mother told her firmly. "It's *much* too expensive. You may have a little milk and prune juice, I can see the sense of that, but no viosterol or dextrose or egg yolk, no siree." Joan sighed. It did sound rather complicated.

"Will prune juice and milk be enough?" she asked.

"That'll be plenty," said Mother. "You watch and see."
So the beautiful formula went into the wastepaper basket.

Joan found that the baby squirrel loved the mixture of
prune juice and milk. Joan filled a medicine dropper with
it and all the children whooped with delight when the
squirrel put both front paws around it and sucked greed-
ily. Joan helped by squeezing the rubber tip a little. The
squirrel drank three medicine droppers full, left a few
funny little black droppings on Joan's palm and went to
sleep, curled up in his blanket.

"I guess we ought to put him in the screened porch
upstairs," Joan told Mother. "He has to be outside, Mr.
Hollis says, and I'm afraid of cats. May I sleep in the porch
too and keep him company?"

"All right; change places with Peter for a while, if you
like," Mother agreed.

"What are you going to call him?" asked Patsy. " 'Silver' would be a nice name."

"No, 'Silver' is a horse," cried Peter and proposed
"Fluffy," but nobody liked that name either. Angela
finally christened the little squirrel by calling him
"Blinkie" with such assurance that Blinkie he became
forthwith.

Joan felt blissful watching over her pet. Daddy
wouldn't mind, she thought. One little squirrel didn't
make a zoo. With a sigh of happiness she gave Blinkie his
second meal.

When Mr. Spencer came home late after his work, he
heard all about the sixth Mitchell baby. He always sat in
Grannie's room for a while, to talk over the day's happen-
ings and listen to the news. Joan showed Blinkie to him
and he remarked that he had never seen a finer squirrel
baby; it was sure to be the image of its father. Joan

thought so too. Squirrels look rather alike anyway. Meanwhile, Patsy had climbed on Mr. Spencer's knee and sobbed out her distress at her short hair. But Mr. Spencer could not agree with her.

"I'll show you two princess with short hair," he said, taking a photograph of Princess Elizabeth and Princess Margaret Rose from his vest pocket.

"They are my own princesses," he said fondly. "They are the princesses of England and one of them may be a queen one day. Now, do they have long hair?"

Patsy examined the picture carefully.

"They have no crowns," she remarked.

"They don't need them," said Mr. Spencer. "Everyone knows they are princesses."

"Oh." Patsy took it in slowly. Then she blushed and a smile kindled her face.

"Oh! And I am just like them! Oh, isn't it *merciful?* Thank you so much for telling me, Mr. Spencer," she cried, embracing him.

That night when the moon came up and peeped into the Mitchell home to see if everyone was properly tucked in, it smiled down on two very happy little girls.

EIGHT

The Princess

THE next morning Joan was waked early by the birds
and she remembered that she was sleeping on the
porch. She immediately jumped up and looked at Blinkie.
He was well, but very hungry. As she fed him, Joan
wondered what to do with him while she was at school.
He should be fed often, but she dare not bother Mother
with him too much for fear she might not be allowed to
keep him. Perhaps if she dipped a little bread in milk and
left it in his cage, he would be able to suck from it whenever he liked. This proved a good idea. Blinkie even
preferred the soaked bread to the medicine dropper because it was soft and he could dig his paws into it. This
problem solved, Joan had to hurry to get ready for school.

Peter and Patsy had already gone down. Joan found her clothes neatly laid out for her by Mother. As she dressed she wondered what teacher she would have this year, where her classroom would be, and what new children she'd get to know. She badly wanted a "bosom friend," for she'd never really had one. Not the kind you read about in books who share secrets and make pacts and would be glad to die for you. Her friends were all hopelessly casual. Joan felt that though they liked her, they'd just as soon play with some other girl. Perhaps Joan wasn't the sort of person who inspired a special friendship. She studied herself in the mirror. She did look rather ordinary with a round face, a nose of no particular shape and gray eyes of middling size. Joan sighed. She wished she were the kind of person called "exquisite." She wondered what "exquisite" really meant. Lots of nice words started with "e." There was "elegant," "elfin," "eerie," "elusive," "ethereal," and "slender," which didn't start with "e" but was an "e'ish" kind of word. Joan, on the contrary, was the kind of person of whom people said: "My, isn't she healthy looking?" or "What a hearty eater," or "She looks hardy." Nothing but "h's." Joan would much rather have been an "e" girl.

There was Mother calling; Joan would have to hurry or she'd be late the first day. As she stamped downstairs, two steps at a time, Patsy and Peter called out to her that the postman had brought letters.

"From Daddy!" they cried. "And Uncle Jim!"

"Here is yours," said Mother, handing Joan a card. "Daddy sent you all one. Timmy has eaten his already." Joan took the card with interest. It had a war dog on it.

"Dear Joan," it said. "I know you will like this picture. I hear dogs are doing fine in the Army. I'm glad I joined the

Navy. Remember, when I come home from the war I don't want to start fighting dogs, so keep them out of our house, that's a good girl. Study your piano instead. Love, Daddy."

"Oh, Mother," sighed Joan. "Do you think Daddy will object to Blinkie?"

"No," said Mother. "Why should he? Blinkie isn't a dog, and anyway, he stays outside, doesn't he?"

Yes, that was true, and Joan's conscience was reassured. She hadn't really ever *asked* Daddy whether he liked squirrels. She knew he didn't like mice and dogs and fleas and spiders and caterpillars and frogs and angleworms and flies and moths and ants and wasps and cockroaches. But it was quite possible that he had a secret passion for squirrels.

"Let me see your cards," she asked of the other children. Of course Timmy couldn't show his, but Peter had an airplane, Patsy a gremlin, and Angela a ship. All of them had affectionate messages.

Meanwhile Mother was reading one of those funny letters—V-mail—from Daddy, and Grannie was deep in one from Uncle Jim. Mr. Spencer had mail from home, too. They were all so absorbed they didn't even hear the children's "good-by" when they left for school.

It was a sparkling September morning with that little bite in the air which in the end shrivels up the leaves. As the children walked past the White Elephant they hushed their steps. They were very scared of Henry. He always pelted them with acorns whenever he caught sight of them. Yet the White Elephant drew them as a magnet; they just couldn't help it. Now they looked over the hedge.

"I guess nobody is up yet. I don't see anybody, do you?" asked Joan, peering around.

"Maybe Henry went to school already," said Peter.

"Let's sneak in and see what he did to our clubhouse," proposed Joan, who was simply longing to find out if it was still intact.

They crawled through a gap in the hedge and stole to the little house. But when they looked through its window, which was easy to do, for the muslin had been torn down, they saw nothing but a mess.

"They are using it to store things," snorted Patsy.

"I guess that bicycle is Henry's, and those baseball bats and that tennis racket. I guess it's Henry's house all right, only he doesn't know what to do with it," cried Joan indignantly. Suddenly she gasped as a small, withered, wiry old woman with a big nose, piercing black eyes and a very round back shuffled through the brushwood.

"I thought I heard voices," she croaked. "Get out of here, children; this ain't public property. . . . We don't want all the kids of the neighborhood traipsing about the place. Off, off with you, I say!" And she waved a gnarled stick at them. The children ran off as fast as they could, only stopping when they had safely reached the sidewalk.

"A witch!" cried Peter, his eyes round as silver dollars. "A real witch!" The children gazed at one another with breathless wonder.

"Perhaps she'll put a spell on the garden and then, if we set foot in it, we'll turn into an animal," whispered Patsy. "I hope it isn't a dog, for then Daddy won't like me any more. I'd rather be a squirrel and keep Blinkie company."

"Perhaps she has changed some children already," said Peter, relishing the horror of the thought. "Perhaps those sparrows over there are Dickie and Tilly."

But Joan smashed that hope. "I saw them go to school this morning," she said. "And those sparrows look much too comfortable to be newly changed. Anyway, I don't believe there are witches any more."

"What happened to them then?" asked Patsy. "There used to be."

"They died out, or something, I guess," said Joan.

"The stupid ones might have, but the clever ones wouldn't," insisted Patsy. "Has anyone ever *counted* them?"

"I don't think so," Joan admitted.

"Well then," cried Patsy triumphantly. "How do we know who lives in all those houses? Think of it, house after house after house, millions of them. Nobody goes around to look into every single house; there might easily be magicians or witches hiding somewhere."

At that moment a bell rang, reminding the children to hurry. School was in the usual confusion that first day. The children were well content, however. At three o'clock they ran home by the short-cut, a tortuous way leading through all sorts of lenient people's backyards, to tell Mother which teacher they had and which room they were in. Peter got most of her attention because he had never been to the "big school" yet. He acted very grown-up about it, however.

"Oh, it's all right," he said when Mother and Grannie wanted to "hear everything."

Joan was in the sixth grade now and had got the nicest teacher again. Patsy said it wasn't true; she, Patsy, had a much nicer teacher. Joan thought it kinder not to disillusion her, though she knew better. They were all so occupied with their new grades that they had forgotten about the White Elephant.

But the next day on their way from school they had an
adventure. As they passed the White Elephant they saw a
small person walking through the tall grass in the yard.
She wore a rose-colored satin gown which touched the
ground, and a white veil fastened around the head with a
sparkling band.

"She *must* be a princess," said Joan. "She's too big for a
fairy."

"Let's ask," suggested Peter, and before the others
could stop him, he cried, "Hi ya!"

"Sh!" warned Patsy. "You don't say 'Hi ya' to a princess." But Her Highness had heard and came toward
them gravely, holding up her skirts with both hands and
teetering a little on her high-heeled slippers.

"How do you do?" she said with a foreign flavor to her
voice.

"Very well," Joan answered. "I'm Joan, this is Patsy,
and that's Peter. Who are you?"

"Oh." The girl looked thoughtfully at them, her blue
eyes full of mystery.

"I'm . . . it's a secret. No one really knows who I am."

"I know, you are a princess," said Patsy immediately.

The girl's pretty little pointed face warmed into a smile.

"How did you know?" she cried.

"We guessed right away," explained Patsy. "We know
a lot about princesses and you look just like one. Why did
you come here?"

"Oh . . ." the blue eyes clouded again as a shadow stole
over the royal countenance.

"Some of my people didn't want me to be queen," she
explained hurriedly, "and now I have to hide."

"I bet it was Hitler," guessed Peter.

But the princess shook her head quickly. "No, no," she

said. "Not that old Hitler. And anyway, the prince will fetch me back, I know he will. He wants to marry me."

"You're too young to marry," said Joan. "You're younger than I am even."

"Oh, that doesn't matter; princesses can marry as young as they please because they don't have to do any work," Her Highness answered airily.

"Una!" cried a voice from the house. "Oh, Uuuunnna!" The princess seemed to shrink a little inside her finery.

"That's Mrs. Trotter," she said, rapidly dropping her royal tone and sounding like an ordinary little girl. "I'd better go now." And picking up her skirts she ran off, looking rather forlorn for a person of so much importance.

"Mother, there's a girl at the White Elephant who says she is a princess," the children told their mother as soon as they entered the house. "She was chased out of her own country."

"Is that true?" said Mother, looking surprised. "Well, I guess it *could* happen. There are a lot of royal refugees coming over here, but I hadn't expected to see one in our street."

"There is one now," said Peter, "but she is kind of silly." And he was off to play with Dickie.

Joan and Patsy, however, settled down in the hammock together and discussed the possibilities of their royal neighbor.

"Isn't she beautiful?" said Joan. "I can't understand why she is called 'Una.' Her name should have started with an 'e.'" Patsy knew about Joan's letter-theory and nodded.

" 'Princess' Una sounds good, though," she remarked. "I wonder how she gets along with Henry."

"I bet he teases her," said Joan. "I'm sorry for her."

"Perhaps she'll be our friend," murmured Patsy thoughtfully. "I wish she could be in our club."

"We have five members already," Joan reminded her.

"Look, there's Tilly. Hi, Tilly!"

"Hi!" answered Tilly, who was coming up the front steps, clasping a fish bowl. Her eyes were red with weeping.

"What happened?" Joan and Patsy cried together.

"We're moving," Tilly sobbed, and a fat tear splashed into the fish bowl, frightening the gold fish. "We're leaving tomorrow early. I came to say good-by. And we can't take these fishes; Father says it would be too awkward. Do you think your mother would let you have them?"

"Sure," said Joan. "We'd *love* them. Where are you moving to?"

"Some other place," said Tilly in a hollow voice. "I bet I won't have a single friend there and no club or *anything*." She handed the fish bowl to Joan, dug a handkerchief out of her pocket, and blew her nose hard.

"I'll miss you all," she said hoarsely.

"We'll miss you, too," Joan and Patsy assured her warmly.

"Take care of the fishes," Tilly continued anxiously. "The yellow one is called 'Goldy' and the pale one is 'Starlet.' They like the crumbly fish food better than the wafery kind. I *do* wish we didn't have to leave them. You'll be kind to them, won't you? I'm afraid they'll miss me." And more tears slipped out of Tilly's eyes.

Patsy put an arm around her shoulders to comfort her and Joan promised her that she'd take good care of the pets.

"They like to be sung to, sometimes," stammered Tilly, now completely overcome with grief. "G . . . good luck to you all and the c . . . club . . . G . . . good-by. . . ." And tearing herself out of Patsy's embrace, she ran down the steps crying as if her heart would break.

Patsy's eyes were full of tears as she watched after her friend, and Joan felt something tickle in her nose, but she couldn't blow it because of the fish bowl in her arms.

"Poor Tilly," said Patsy. "She'll never see the White Elephant again and she doesn't even know there is a princess."

"It's a good thing we didn't tell her," said Joan. "It would only have made it harder for her." Then she ran indoors to show Mother the gold fish.

"Goodness," said Mother. "Where did you get those?"

"Tilly gave them to us. She is going away and couldn't take them. Do you think Daddy will mind?"

"No, of course not," said Mother. "Fishes are no trouble at all."

And so the fish bowl was put on the sideboard in the dining room and the Mitchell household was blessed with two more pets.

NINE

Una Wendell

PRINCESS UNA was a very mysterious person, the children decided. They didn't see half enough of her, though they peeped through and over the hedge as often as they could, only taking care that Henry or the witch didn't see them.

They now definitely believed she *was* a witch, who kept the princess captive. Peter felt much more interested in the witch than in the princess and would go to the most elaborate precautions not to be "magicked." He'd carry a raw potato, or hold a blessed medal, or walk backwards, or keep his fingers crossed; every day he invented something different. But the girls had come to the conclusion that witches wouldn't last long if they started to cast spells about in the street. Since the stupid witches could reasonably be supposed extinct by now, this must be a clever one who wouldn't attempt anything so crude. They were much more afraid of her effect on the princess, who was evidently in her power. They saw the princess one morning, dressed in a black frock and perched on the high limb of a tree.

"I guess she is being changed into a crow," suggested Patsy.

"Oh my goodness," said Joan.

But Peter told them not to worry; he knew a countercharm which was sure to work. All they had to do was to hop to school, three hops and a skip, and sing "Crow away, Princess come," all the time, over and over. The girls tried it, but were shy of doing it near school. Peter didn't care; he continued to the bitter end, and when a boy laughed at him, he dealt him a sock on the jaw. Peter wasn't going to have any little girl changed into a crow if he could help it, no siree.

On the way home he was pleased to see his charm had worked, for Una was sitting quietly in the grass, reading a book. But suddenly he realized that he had been foolish in specifying a crow. The witch might decide to change the princess into some other animal. So for the rest of the way he continued to hop and skip, singing "Animals away, Princess come," for safety's sake.

The girls left school a little later than Peter, and when they passed the White Elephant the princess was not alone any more. Henry was with her, and he had grabbed her book, holding it out of reach.

"Oh, please give it back," pleaded Una in her gentlest

voice. "Please do, Henry. I've just got to the part where the 'little mermaid' gets her legs."

"What do you want to read stuff like that for?" teased Henry. "And out of such a filthy old book, too. Look at it." And holding it between his thumb and forefinger, he pulled a face at it.

It did look like an old book; some of the pages threatened to drop out from between the covers. There was a shriek of anguish from the princess.

"It's not filthy and it can't help being old," she cried, stretching out her arms. "Please give it back to me, Henry; it is my very own, it is the only thing that is my very own!"

"Pooh, you can't have anything of your very own yet," said Henry. "You're only a minor and you're too scatterbrained anyway. You'd be much better off without the book. I think I'll throw it away."

And with a teasing grin he made as if to fling the book into the bushes. But he didn't count on Joan, who had been watching the scene with mounting indignation and now leaped over the hedge.

"Give that book back *at once*," she cried, fists clenched, eyes flashing. "Give it back at once! Hear?"

"So, it's you, Smarty," said Henry, lifting his eyebrows as if excessively surprised. "My, my, what a pother you are in. Don't you remember what I told you about keeping off my property?" And he scowled fiercely, making a motion as if to hit her.

But Joan was much too angry to be frightened. "I'm not scared of you," she shouted. "You're nothing but a big bully who likes to tease girls, but if I were a boy you'd run like a hare. I can fight, too, much better than you think! If you dare to hit me I'll scratch you and kick you and bite you and pull out your hair. And my brother and sister will help me."

"Yes!" cried Peter and Patsy, safely sheltered by the hedge.

"So you give that book back right away, do you *hear?*"

Henry was a little nonplussed; Joan did look rather formidable in her fury. He noticed that she was a muscular little girl. The one thing Henry hated was to be made ridiculous. And it would certainly be ridiculous if he were to fight a younger girl and be conquered. Besides, Henry wasn't very fond of fighting. He only enjoyed making others uncomfortable as long as it cost him nothing.

"All right, I was only kidding anyway," he said gruffly. "You girls never can take a bit of fun." And tossing the book into Una's lap, he sauntered off with his hands in his pockets, whistling a careless tune.

"Oh, *thank* you," cried Una fervently, looking at Joan with eyes which sparkled with tears. "My own, precious book!" And she clasped it against her heart as if it were a doll. "I've had this book as long as I can remember," she told Joan solemnly. "I think I'd *die* if something happened to it. Thank you so much for making Henry give it back to me. I'm going to hide it where he can't find it." And quick as a fairy she ran off to the house. Joan crawled through the hedge to join Peter and Patsy, who had been watching her with speechless admiration.

Mother was puzzled by the children's account of the new neighbors at the White Elephant. At first she had thought they might be refugees. Refugees had to live somewhere, so why not there? But all this talk of witches and magic seemed strange. She wished she had time to pay a visit there and find out, but her days were packed full with necessary duties. Shopping took so long nowa-

days, and it was hard to lug the groceries. Mother sighed for the time when you could just telephone and have everything delivered.

One morning she was wheeling her purchases home, balanced precariously around Timmy in his buggy, while Angela tagged after her, clasping a loaf of bread. They were just passing the White Elephant house when a wheel jumped off the carriage and rolled down the sidewalk. Timmy almost fell out of the lurching buggy. A box of cookies and a can of beans did fall.

"Angela, pick up the wheel!" cried Mother, trying to hold on to Timmy, rescue the food and steady the carriage at the same time, an impossible undertaking.

Timmy was frightened and started to cry, and Angela said she couldn't find the wheel. So Mother took Timmy in her arms, left the wrecked buggy, and helped Angela look for the wheel. But when she had it she didn't know how to put it back. She could not let go of Timmy for fear he should march into traffic; he refused to return to the treacherous stroller, and with him in her arms she couldn't replace the wheel. Suddenly a lady ran out of the White Elephant.

"I saw you struggling and I thought you needed help," she said. She was a rather large person with a florid, handsome face and a voluble tongue.

"She can't be the witch," thought Mother. Aloud she only said: "Oh, it's just the wheel came off. Please, don't bother!"

"Indeed I *shall* bother," said the lady. "The idea of leaving you to struggle right in front of my house. Give me that wheel!"

"Really, you shouldn't," murmured Mother, but the lady paid no attention and knelt right down to fix the wheel with a bobby pin.

"Thank you *so* much," said Mother gratefully, but the lady laughed.

"Neighbors is neighbors," she said. "If the Lord didn't expect us to help each other, what *did* He expect us to do? I've been wanting to meet you; I've seen you pass by on the street quite a few times. My name is Abigail Trotter."

"And I'm Rita Mitchell," answered Mother, shaking hands.

"Come and sit on my porch for a minute," proposed Mrs. Trotter. "I can see you've been doing a lot of shopping; you must be tired. What cute little children you have."

"I've three more," said Mother proudly.

"Oh, my goodness, I guess they keep you busy, don't they? I always wanted a lot of children but I have only the one boy. He is at school at present. Pf, isn't it hot, though? Up north the leaves are turning already, but it's summer here yet. Sit down, Mrs. Mitchell, and make yourself comfortable. Oh, don't worry about the little boy; he can't do any harm here."

"Thank you," said Mother, sitting down in the rocking chair Mrs. Trotter held out for her.

"Isn't it hard to find a house here?" Mrs. Trotter went on. "When my husband was called up, I took a position with the Government and had to come and live here, though I hated to leave my home in the Adirondacks. We built it ourselves and Henry was born there. This house is much too large, but I've rented some rooms to nice, quiet people and that helps out."

"That's just what I did," said Mother.

"The trouble is the yard," Mrs. Trotter went on. "It's such a large yard and it's full of poison ivy and weeds, and the grass is so high I'm afraid of ticks. But I can't seem to find anyone to clean it up for me."

"My children could help you, perhaps," suggested Mother. "They have a club that does that sort of thing and a few war stamps would make them very happy." She had difficulty in talking, for Timmy was struggling to get off her lap. Angela leant shyly against her mother's shoulder.

"Oh, that would be wonderful," cried Mrs. Trotter. "Send them over to me, will you? How do you manage so many children? I've always found my one boy a handful, and now with Una here I sometimes am at my wit's end. Una is the little refugee who is staying with us," she explained.

Mother tried not to show her curiosity. "I heard about her," she said. "A little princess, isn't she?"

Mrs. Trotter shook her head. "Nobody knows who she is. She was brought over here in a boat from Portugal. She must be English, because that is the only language she knows, but no one has been able to locate her parents. According to the Refugee Committee she must have come from France. But the child was badly upset by her experiences and they weren't able to get much information from her. As a matter of fact, she was sent to a special school when she first arrived, to get adjusted. But she didn't thrive there and the authorities decided that a private home would be better for her. She is a peculiar child; I don't understand her very well. She is full of strange fancies. There is a dirty old book which she seems to have clung to through all her travels and she just can't bear to part with it. Henry hasn't taken to her at all. He says she is too fairyfied. It is true that she seems to have difficulty in separating fact from fiction, and I'm trying to get her to have a little common sense. But it's uphill work." Mrs. Trotter heaved a deep sigh. "I would have preferred to adopt a boy," she mused. "I had wanted a companion for Henry."

"Henry is much older than Una, isn't he?" remarked Mother.

"Yes, and I'm afraid he resents having a girl in the house, which makes it all rather difficult," said Mrs. Trotter. "I do so want this unfortunate child to be happy at last. But I have to consider Henry, too; he has first rights." Mother agreed that it was hard for her.

"Of course, I haven't decided to keep Una permanently yet," explained Mrs. Trotter. "She is only here on probation. The Committee won't let you adopt anyone unless it's reasonably sure to work."

"That is very wise," nodded Mother.

"The child's health is a problem, too," continued Mrs. Trotter, who seemed glad of a chance to unburden herself. "The doctor won't let her go to school yet. He wants her to play outdoors a lot. Of course, I can't look after her in the daytime because I have my work, but luckily I took our faithful Hanna with me. It is a big responsibility all the same." And Mrs. Trotter frowned.

Angela thought she was frowning at her and bristled up. "I'm *good*," she announced to the world in general. Mrs. Trotter's face relaxed a little.

"Yes you are, honey, you're a sweety pie," she admitted generously.

"Then put away that stick," Angela commanded.

"Which stick?" Mrs. Trotter held up her hands to show they were empty.

"That one." And Angela pointed to the wrinkle between Mrs. Trotter's eyebrows. Mrs. Trotter began to laugh.

"Yes, I guess I *do* frown," she admitted humbly. "You remind me when you see it, little girl. Would you like some orangeade?"

"Yes!" cried Angela, clapping her hands.

"All right then, we'll have Hanna bring us some. Hanna!" cried Mrs. Trotter.

As Hanna came out on the porch Mother realized she must be the "witch" from the looks of her. Presently the orangeade arrived in tall glasses with tinkling ice cubes inside. Timmy stretched out his arms for it. Mrs. Trotter gave him a glassful and he drank it with an absorbed expression. He drank and drank until it was all gone except a little dribble down his chin. He looked thoughtfully at the empty glass in his hand, and before Mother could stop him he had heaved it up and smashed it on the floor.

"Oh, dear," cried Mother, much embarrassed, but Mrs. Trotter told her it didn't matter.

"It was only one of those little jelly glasses you get free." And she bent to pick up the pieces.

At that moment a curious personage mounted the porch steps from the garden. She was dressed in blue slacks with a red silk scarf tied around her middle and feathers stuck in her long red curls which radiantly framed her pale little face. What interested Mother most were her eyes. Wide and blue, they had a look as if they'd seen beyond death and hadn't quite forgotten.

"There's Una now," said Mrs. Trotter. "Oh, my dear, you shouldn't have taken that scarf out of my room; it's my best one and real silk is so hard to get now. Why didn't you ask me first?" Una cast down her eyes, her long, curved, gold-tipped lashes sweeping her cheeks.

"Well, Una, why didn't you? Don't you remember what you promised me last time?" Mrs. Trotter insisted gently.

"I'm not Una," murmured the girl. "I'm Hiawatha."

Mrs. Trotter frowned.

"Come, come, Una, none of that nonsense," she said. "You know very well you are not Hiawatha but Una Wendell. Hiawatha has been dead long ago, if he ever existed. Where did you get that notion?"

Una's face closed like a flower at sundown. "It was in a book," she said dully. "In your bookcase."

Mother's heart warmed to the child, and stretching out her hand, she took Una's slender fingers in hers. "I know the book you mean," she said. "I used to love to read it when I was a little girl. He had a wonderful father, hadn't he? A father who ruled the winds of Heaven. . . ." Una nodded brightly.

"Yes, his father could do anything!" she cried, flashing up her blue eyes with their moving expression and gazing gratefully at Mother's understanding face:

"I wish I had a father like that . . ." she added softly.

"You must come to visit us soon," Mother went on, gently patting the little hand she held. "I am the mother of some children you've met already, I think. Two girls and a little boy."

"Oh, are you *Joan's* mother?" asked Una eagerly. "Oh, I'd *love* to come! May I, Mrs. Trotter?"

"We'll see what the doctor says," Mrs. Trotter told her. "Now you'd better go up and put that scarf back and tidy yourself. I've got some orangeade and cookies here for you."

"Oh, thank you," cried Una and ran into the house. Mother watched her thoughtfully.

"She seems a nice child," she said.

"Oh yes," Mrs. Trotter agreed. "She is nice enough, but I don't understand her and I wish she and Henry would get along better."

"Perhaps they'll get used to each other after a while," Mother consoled her. "I'm afraid I have to be going now, the children will be coming home for lunch soon. I do thank you for your hospitality and help."

"Oh, you're welcome, I'm sure," said Mrs. Trotter. "I'm glad I was home. I usually work during the day, but I have to go to the dentist this afternoon so I thought I'd take the day off." She accompanied Mother to the sidewalk and shook hands with her cordially.

"It was so interesting to talk to you," she said. "Drop in again when you pass by."

"I'd love to," murmured Mother, putting Timmy in his stroller.

"Don't forget to send the children to clean up the yard," Mrs. Trotter reminded her.

"No, I won't. Good-by now."

"Bye! Bye!" cried Angela.

Mother walked home slowly, thinking of poor little Una Wendell. She thought it must be terrible for a child not to have people of her own to depend on. No matter how kind strangers were, it was never the same. Of course, Mother knew that adopted children could be made happy, and perhaps Una was lucky to have found a kind home. But all the same, Mother couldn't forget the tragic look in Una's eyes.

"War is terrible," she muttered.

The children felt very excited when, coming home from school, they heard about Mother's adventures. A little orphan refugee from Hitler seemed even more romantic to them than a princess. And when they heard that Mrs. Trotter wanted her yard cleaned, they decided that it was definitely a job for the club. So they called a meeting in Tilly's empty house and agreed to present themselves at the White Elephant next Saturday morning.

"But what about the witch?" asked Peter.

"She isn't a witch; she's a maid called Hanna," explained Joan.

But Peter and Patsy didn't believe it, and because they didn't, Dickie didn't either. Joan missed Tilly, who had always been on her side.

"A witch could be a servant," Patsy was saying. "She'd have to be *something* to get into people's houses."

"I know what," said Peter. "We'll put salt in our pockets and then nothing can happen." But Joan assured him she would do no such thing, the idea!

TEN

At the White Elephant

O N SATURDAY morning the club, equipped with a
wheelbarrow, a big lawn rake, a lawn mower, a pair of
shears and the beloved flag, marched to the White Elephant's yard. Mrs. Trotter met the children at the gate.
She was dressed in her best hat and coat and announced
that she was going into town with Henry. Henry was
beside her in a new suit, his hair slicked down under his
cap.

"The grass is most important," explained Mrs. Trotter.
"And of course, if you could clip the hedge, that would be
wonderful. You'll all get three war stamps if you make the
place look tidy. Hanna will show you what to do with the
rubbish."

"Where is Una, couldn't Una help, too?" asked Joan eagerly.

Mrs. Trotter shook her head. "I'm afraid Una has to stay in her room today," she said. "I had to punish her, much as I disliked to, but she behaved rather badly."

Mrs. Trotter kindly refrained from mentioning Una's offense, but Henry immediately drawled: "She broke my mother's *best* mirror," in a tone of lofty disapproval.

Joan felt he wasn't in the least sorry about the mirror; only pleased that Una should have made his mother angry, and she disliked him more than ever.

"Well, we must be going now," said Mrs. Trotter. "Good-by, children; do your best." And she and Henry hurried down the street to catch a bus.

"Now we must divide the work," said Joan, taking charge like an officer. "You pick up the paper and rubbish, Peter, but watch out for poison ivy. Throw all the trash in the cart and ask Hanna where to dump it. Patsy may cut off the long grass with the shears and Dickie has to rake it away. I'll follow up with the lawn mower."

So said, so done. The children were soon happily occupied, and the sunny air rang with their voices. One of the bedroom windows of the White Elephant swung open and Una leaned out.

"Hello," she cried.

"Hi!" said Joan, stopping the lawn mower a moment.

"I have to stay in," said Una. "I've been falsely accused of a crime and The Queen has locked me up in the tower. My hair isn't long enough to let myself down by, either," she finished mournfully.

"Didn't you break the mirror?" asked Joan.

"No," said Una. "How did you know it *was* a mirror?"

"Henry told us," Joan explained.

"He ought to know," Una remarked coldly. "He did it himself."

"Then why didn't you *say* so?" Joan called back indignantly.

"Because . . . because I'm scared of Henry," admitted Una, almost in a whisper. Then she added quickly:

"Anyway, it doesn't matter. I'd much rather be a princess, locked in a tower."

"Would you like to be rescued?" asked Joan.

"I'd love it!" cried Una. "But the door is locked."

"Oh, we can take care of that," Joan promised. "You wait." She deliberated for a moment with the other club members.

"The only worry is Hanna," she said. "She'll notice it if we rescue Una. You'll have to keep her busy, Peter." Peter shuddered.

"I will," offered Dickie.

"I'll go with you," said Peter. He remembered that he had filled his pockets so full of salt nothing could happen to him.

"You two go and talk to her then, while Patsy and I get Una out of her room."

"But what'll we do when Hanna sees her in the garden later?" asked Patsy. Joan thought it over.

"I know; we'll dress her up and pretend she is Tilly. You run home and get your blue overalls and that big sun hat of Peter's. When she has that on, no one will be able to see her face. And also get the ladder out of our garage."

"I won't be able to carry all that," protested Patsy, so Joan decided to go with her.

Meanwhile Peter and Dickie went to visit Hanna. Hanna was washing clothes in the basement. The boys offered to hang them up for her. That would keep her from going into the yard and watching what was happening there. Hanna was surprisingly grateful. She said she wasn't as young as she used to be and could do with a little help. Peter and Dickie felt pleased that they didn't have to talk. Conversation with a witch was bound to be awkward, they thought. You never knew what subjects to avoid. Surely one should never mention broomsticks, or cats, or pumpkins? There might be hundreds of other sore subjects they didn't know about and talking might get them into trouble, as it did Alice in Wonderland when she kept saying things about her cat to the mouse. Hanging up clothes was a lot easier.

Joan and Patsy had some trouble carrying the heavy ladder, but at last they arrived with it at the White Elephant. It was just long enough to reach Una's window and Joan found she could easily climb into the room. Una quickly changed into the clothes Joan had brought her and then Joan helped her descend the ladder. Afterward they hid the ladder under some bushes, and then the three girls took one another by the hand and danced around.

"Lovely!" cried Joan. "Now you are Tilly, Una, and you'd better do some work, too. Help me push the mower; it's pretty heavy. If you see anyone, bend your head; then your hat hides your face."

Una was smiling with joy. Instead of having to spend a whole day in dreary and undeserved loneliness, she was out in the sunshine with *friends*.

"I love being rescued," she said. "I wish I could *stay* rescued." Joan threw her a swift glance.

"Don't you like it here?" she asked.

"Oh yes," said Una immediately. "Mrs. Trotter is very

nice. But I should like most to be a princess and live with people I loved."

Patsy gazed thoughtfully at her.

"We're not princesses but we do live with people we love," she said. "I thought you always *had* to love the people you lived with."

"Even Henry?" asked Una incredulously.

"We have to love our enemies," murmured Patsy.

"Oh, that's easy," cried Una. "You do not see your enemies very often. Henry is different." Joan and Patsy thought it over.

"We have to love our neighbor, too," Joan pointed out.

"Oh!" Una cheered up immediately. "You are my neighbors, aren't you? That's all right then, for I love you truly." And she gazed ecstatically from Joan to Patsy.

Peter and Dickie had, by now, hung up all the light laundry and Hanna herself came out to hang the sheets. Peter pinched Dickie in his arm and Dickie cried: "Ouch!" but Hanna glanced only for a moment at the three girls working in the garden. She didn't remember having seen the one with the big hat before, but children were always hopping about, now you saw them, then you didn't. It left Hanna cold.

"What's that you've got in your pocket?" she asked. Peter had forgotten his salt. It was leaking out of one of his pockets.

"You didn't go pinching my sugar, did you?" asked Hanna severely.

"No, it's salt," said Peter. Then he realized that it was a stupid thing to say. Hanna might guess why he had put it there and be offended. But Hanna apparently didn't.

"Salt?" she said, genuinely surprised. "What do you

carry salt for?" Now Peter was in a fix. What was he to say? But Dickie rescued him.

"To catch birds with," he said stolidly, not a flicker of an eyelid showing it was a joke. "You put some on their tails," he explained elaborately. Peter hid his face. He wasn't as clever at controlling his features as Dickie.

Hanna snorted. "Get along with you, you're too old to believe them stories," she said. "Run off, both of you; you've helped me enough, I don't want to be helped to a headache. You ought to be clearing up the garden, anyway." And grumpily Hanna descended the cellar steps to fetch more sheets.

As soon as Joan saw the boys saunter back over the grass she motioned them to be still.

"There's a little baby bunny in the yard," she whispered. "Quite a wee one! We're trying to catch him."

"A *real* one?" asked Peter, crouching down beside Joan.

"Of course," said Patsy. "We wouldn't have to catch a toy one. There, I saw him, Una, quick!" The plumes of the uncut part of the lawn waved about and the children saw the tips of two brown ears. Dickie darted behind Una and made a grab at them.

"I've got him!" he cried, holding a tiny grayish brown bunny in his hands. It squirmed and kicked.

"Oh, don't hurt him," cried Una. "Give him to me."

"Don't let him escape then," warned Dickie. "He is mighty quick."

Una held the struggling bunny in her arms and put her cheek against its soft fur. Her eyes glowed.

"Could I keep him?" she pleaded. "He is so sweet. I've never had a pet."

"Of course you can keep him," said Joan. "He was in your yard."

"It's Henry's yard and Henry will want him," Una argued gently. "I wish I could do magic; then I'd make him invisible. Would it be wrong to hide him, please? I could keep him in a drawer. One of them has a hole where the knob came off." Joan laughed.

"You'd need something bigger than a drawer for that bunny," she said. "I know what: we've got some bushel-baskets at home. Let's fetch one. Peter, you go. Mother has promised us a picnic, so bring food at the same time."

"Good," said Peter. "I'm terribly hungry. Come, Dickie."

Peter and Dickie ran off and the girls chose a place for their picnic, an open spot between trees where the grass had been cut. The children had done a lot that morning, notwithstanding the interruptions. The lawn was smooth and all the rubbish had been carted off to the alley where it would be burnt by Hanna. Patsy and Joan hurriedly finished the last patches of grass while Una played with her bunny, feeding it succulent leaves. Presently Peter and Dickie returned, carrying the basket between them, heaped with provisions.

Joan spread out the napkin Mother had sent, while the boys and Una put the bunny into its new bed. Then Joan parceled out the food and Patsy poured lemonade into paper cups. There were slices of cherry pie, apples, raisin buns and tomato sandwiches. The children ate and ate— Una, too, who said she couldn't remember ever having eaten so much.

"I feel hungry now," she said.

"Didn't you feel hungry when you didn't get enough food, over in Europe?" asked Joan.

Una shook her head. "Only sick," she said.

"Did you ever see a German soldier?" asked Peter

curiously. Una shivered. "Yes." she said. "Please don't talk about it."

"But . . ." began Peter. Joan nudged him.

"We want to talk about our club," she said quickly. "Will you join it, Una?"

"Yes, please," said Una gratefully, brightening again. "What kind of a club? Is it secret?"

"Kind of," said Joan. "You're not to tell Henry, of course."

"I guess I'll have to ask Mrs. Trotter, though," said Una, frowning. "And she doesn't like me to be anything but just Una Wendell."

"But that's what you'll be in the club, too," explained Joan. "We don't change our names or anything. Of course, we have rules. That's our flag there, on the lawn. We bought it with the first money we saved."

"It's the prettiest flag in the street," Peter proclaimed proudly. "I made a V on the stick with a knife, to show it belongs to our club."

"I'm president," said Joan. "But you can be vice president if you like, Una."

"And I then?" asked Dickie. "I'm nothing. Just a *member*." It was an old grievance of his.

"Well, you could be . . . you could be vice treasurer," decided Joan.

Dickie smiled broadly. Vice treasurer sounded even better than treasurer, and he threw a look of triumph at Peter.

Suddenly the peaceful little scene was shattered. A large squirt of water hissed past the branches of a bush and splashed over the tablecloth and the bunny's basket, sending the little creature scurrying around.

"Ouch! ow! ooh!" cried the girls, jumping up. The

stream wobbled back and forth, shooting bullets of water at all the children. They ran out of its reach, but Joan remembered to shout at Una: "Head down."

Una understood and kept hiding her face, but now she couldn't see to avoid the water and she was soon dripping wet. As the children fled, trying to keep under cover, they heard Henry's high laugh.

"Ha! Ha!" he cried. "See them run! The cowards!"

Joan would have loved to turn around and prove to Henry how scared she was, but she had to think of Una. No one must guess that she had been in the yard all morning and on no account must Henry see her face, even if it ruined the Mitchell reputation.

"We can always make up for that later," thought Joan grimly.

She and Patsy were carrying the bushelbasket with Una's pet in it. This rather hampered their movements. Henry was pursuing them, holding the hose in his hand like a gun. He would soon catch up with them.

"The bombshelter," cried Joan.

Patsy understood right away. They were near the place where they had dug it, but it wasn't very noticeable under the twigs and leaves. Joan skirted neatly around it, leaving it an unseen barrier between her and Henry. Henry didn't look at the ground at all, he was too intent on overtaking the girls.

Suddenly he cried "Ouch!" and fell headlong into the concealed pit.

In his confusion he paid no attention to the hose he held, his arm jerked up and the water poured all over Henry himself instead of on his victims. The girls would have liked to admire the gratifying spectacle, but they had to get away as fast as they could for Una's sake. They were

rounding the corner of the house, past the cellar steps, when Hanna popped her head out of the basement door and beckoned them inside. Peter hurriedly felt in his pockets, but all the salt had been washed away by the water. The others, however, had already followed Hanna into the cellar, so Peter thought he'd better go, too. As soon as they were inside Hanna locked the door.

"Don't look so scared," she said. "I know what happened. Master Henry was at his tricks again. A nice way to treat a bunch of friendly kids who come to help his mother! But teasing is in his blood; I've known him for twelve years now. Take off those wet things before you get sick. I'll iron them dry for you. Here is a bunch of towels to wrap around you. You, too, Una. Yes, I knew all along it was you. Hanna may be old but she hasn't lost her eyesight yet. And mind you, I wouldn't have let you sneak out of your punishment if I hadn't been sure that it was Henry who broke that mirror."

"Yes it was, Hanna, truly," said Una.

Hanna's harsh old face softened as she looked at the child.

"I knew it, my pet," she said. "Hanna wasn't born yesterday. Off with these clothes now, all of you. The iron is hot."

"If Hanna isn't a witch," thought Peter, "she must be a fairy godmother." And he gazed at her with admiration as he sat wrapped in his towel, waiting for his suit.

The children learnt that Hanna was a very thorough person. Besides fixing their clothes so that they looked like new, she also kept an eye on Henry, whom she could see through the window, wandering around in his dripping clothes, a big scowl on his face. He was trying to find out where the children had disappeared to so suddenly.

Hanna went outside and called to him: "What ails you?" she cried. "You're all wet. If you don't get into the house and put dry clothes on at once you'll be a sick boy next week and you won't be able to go camping." Henry went grumbling into the house, and the children could hear him stomp upstairs.

"Now it will be all right for you to leave," said Hanna. "That boy has set his heart on going to that camp and he won't dare put his nose out of doors for fear of getting sick. Yes, I'll get Una safely upstairs with no one the wiser. Of course I won't tell Mrs. Trotter. By the way, don't you youngsters go searching for your ladder now; you had hidden it where no one could miss seeing it, so I threw it over the hedge into Dickie's yard and you can fetch it there."

"Oh, Hanna! you're a *darling*," cried Joan.

But Hanna grumbled that she was only a human being; and she never had been able to stand a tease and never would. And she wasn't going to miss a chance of helping a poor little war orphan either, not she. So Una had better come with her while the other children took leave of Mrs. Trotter.

"And my bunny?" asked Una. "What happens to my bunny? May I keep it?" Hanna said she could try, but if Henry found it, it would be just too bad. He would be sure to want it for himself, and he was not always kind to animals.

"What shall I do then?" asked Una, her lips trembling. "Let it go?"

"In the yard?" Hanna shook her head. "No, honey, someone would be sure to find it and kill it."

"Would you like us to take it home and keep it for you?" offered Joan. "We can put it in our screened porch; we have a squirrel there already."

"Oh yes, please. You take it," begged Una, who was then led up a back stairs by Hanna.

The children mounted the cellar steps with the basket. "I think Dickie and Peter ought to take our things home," said Joan. "The bunny, too; it can sit in the cart. Patsy and I'll go and say good-by to Mrs. Trotter."

So it was arranged.

Mrs. Trotter seemed pleased to see the girls.

"Thank you very much; you've done a wonderful job," she said and handed them their war stamps.

The children thanked her, but at that very moment they caught sight of Henry who had entered the hall with dry clothes on. His amazement at seeing the girls in their ironed dresses was so funny that Patsy and Joan grew red as beetroots with suppressed laughter. They hastily took leave of Mrs. Trotter and ran down the porch steps, still looking flushed, when they ran slap bang into . . . Miss Merryvale, of all people!

"Ouch! cried the girls.

"Oooh!" squealed Miss Merryvale, rushing past them with a look of horror and vanishing into Mrs. Trotter's house.

"I bet she still thinks we have scarlet fever," said Patsy. "You *do* look red, Joan."

"And so do you," cried Joan. "What on earth is Miss Merryvale doing here? Let's go home and tell Mother!"

Mother was definitely worried when she heard what had happened.

"Miss Merryvale must have taken a room there," she said. "Mrs. Trotter mentioned that she had roomers."

"Oh dear." The girls looked at each other. "We were just getting so friendly with Una," lamented Joan. "She is going to be a member of our club. You should have told Miss Merryvale right away that she was mistaken."

"I guess I should," Mother admitted. "But it seemed so much simpler . . . who would have thought . . ."

"You must always tell the truth," said Joan virtuously. "You *never* know how things will turn out."

"I don't know what Mrs. Trotter must think of me," murmured Mother. "She'll think it very queer that I didn't tell her about the scarlet fever when I visited her!"

"Wouldn't we have been quarantined if we'd really had scarlet fever?" asked Joan.

"Of course," Mother explained. "They must think we're trying to dodge the law."

"Couldn't we *explain?*" asked Patsy.

"How?" asked Mother. "Do you want me to say:

'Hullo, Miss Merryvale, we believe that you believe that we have scarlet fever but we haven't'? Then Miss Merryvale could say: 'Why didn't you tell me before?' And what am I to say then? 'Oh, Miss Merryvale, we thought it would be simpler'? Or 'We thought you'd be much happier somewhere else'? Or 'We just never got around to it'?" The children laughed at Mother's face when she said this. They realized that it would be awkward for her. Their only hope was that Miss Merryvale had not told Mrs. Trotter.

ELEVEN

Joan Fixes It

MOTHER was really embarrassed by that scarlet fever mix-up. She met Mrs. Trotter coming home from church the next day, but Mrs. Trotter coldly ignored her.

"You should have approached her anyway," Grannie advised afterward. "You should have explained. We can't let Miss Carrytale ruin our relations with our neighbors."

"Merryvale," Mother corrected mechanically, but she knew that Grannie was right.

Joan had her worries, too. Peter and Dickie had forgotten to bring home the flag the day before. It would have been easy to go up to Mrs. Trotter and ask for it—if only Miss Merryvale hadn't complicated things.

"We'll have to fetch it back secretly," Joan decided. So she gathered the club together and they sneaked to the White Elephant's yard.

"You and Dickie will have to keep watch," Joan whispered to Peter. "When you see Henry, whistle once. When you see a grown-up, whistle twice."

Peter and Dickie took up their positions with pride while Joan and Patsy crawled through a hole in the hedge and slinked through the bushes on hands and feet, often halting to listen for suspicious noises. But when they arrived at the place where they had left their flag, it wasn't there any more. They searched around as much as they dared, but it had vanished completely.

"What can have happened?" wondered Patsy.

"I bet Henry took it," grumbled Joan. "It is just like him. I bet he took it when he was chasing us with the hose, and that's why Peter and Dickie didn't bring it. If they'd seen it they would have taken it with them."

The girls looked sadly at the place where the flag had waved so bravely the day before.

"It was an expensive flag, too," murmured Joan mournfully. "It took us a long time to save up for it." Suddenly she lifted her head and clutched Patsy by the arm.

"What's that noise?" she whispered. There was a queer choked sound coming from behind an evergreen tree.

"It sounds like crying," said Patsy. "Let's look." They crept cautiously around the tree and found Una sitting in the grass, sobbing piteously.

"I guess she is sad because we may not play with her," Joan whispered to her sister. Then she let out a low whistle. Una looked up, startled. When she saw the girls she laughed happily.

"Oh, it's you!" she cried. "I was afraid it would be Henry!"

"Hush," warned Joan, "don't shout so. Mrs. Trotter may not see us; she thinks we have scarlet fever." Una nodded.

"I know," she said. "Miss Merryvale told her. Hanna said she didn't believe a word of it. But Miss Merryvale told Mrs. Trotter that it was why she left you and she said a lot more things. Mrs. Trotter says I can't play with you any more and . . . and . . . they took away my book!" Una burst into fresh tears. Joan put an arm across her shoulders.

"Why won't she let you read your book?" she asked.

"Henry saw me reading when I was supposed to be sleeping—he must have looked through the keyhole. He t . . . t . . . told his mother and Miss Merryvale was there, too, and she said no w . . . w . . . wonder I had nightmares, fairy tales were m . . . m . . . most unsuitable for children. Mrs. Trotter believed her and took away my book, my only b . . . b . . . book. . . ." Poor Una sobbed and sobbed. Joan gathered her in her arms.

"There, there," she said soothingly, smothering Una's hair the way she had seen Mother do with Angela. Una was thin, much thinner even than Patsy.

"There, there," said Joan. "You'll get your book back. Mrs. Trotter is only keeping it for you. And we have lovely books to lend you."

"Yes," said Patsy. "And Miss Merryvale can't say anything about them because they are 'unfairy' books."

"Oh." Una rested her head gratefully against Joan's broad shoulder. "*Have* you got scarlet fever?" she asked.

"Of course not," giggled Patsy. "Do you think we'd be here if we had? Mother is most terribly particular about things like that. When we had whooping cough we had to stay in our yard all the time."

"But then . . . why does Miss Merryvale think you have?" asked Una, surprised.

The girls explained the whole mistake and Una forgot her grief as she listened, laughing when Patsy imitated Miss Merryvale's fright at discovering them.

"Why don't *you* explain to Mrs. Trotter?" urged Joan. "Then we can play together again."

"But then Mrs. Trotter would know that Una had spoken to us," Patsy pointed out, "and she might be angry."

"And Mrs. Trotter would think I only imagined it all. She doesn't believe me much," said Una sadly. "She believes Miss Merryvale a lot more."

Joan frowned. It was a silly situation. She wanted so

badly to be friends with Una and now an absurd mistake made it impossible.

"I wish Miss Merryvale wouldn't talk so much," Una went on. "She is always telling Mrs. Trotter how naughty you all are; she even told about your little sister breaking her angel."

"She didn't mean to do that," Joan defended Angela quickly. "She thought it would fly."

Una chuckled. "I wish I could play with her. She is called Angela, isn't she?"

"If you'd only be allowed to visit us," said Joan. "But I guess that's out now." She pondered for a moment. Miss Merryvale seemed to be the main trouble. If only Miss Merryvale would leave. . . .

"I've got it," she cried. "I know what to do. Does Mrs. Trotter come home early on weekdays?"

"No, she doesn't come home until six," said Una. "But Miss Merryvale comes home about four, and Henry at three-thirty, except on Mondays. Then he goes to his music lesson and only comes home at five-thirty. I know, because I never like him to come home," she added feelingly.

"Goody," said Joan. "That suits me fine. Now all I want you to do is to tell Mrs. Trotter that you don't feel well tomorrow. Make her keep you in bed."

"But why?" asked Una. "I hate to be in bed."

"It's part of my plan," Joan told her. "It can't be helped."

Suddenly a piercing whistle roused the girls.

"That's Peter," whispered Joan. "It means someone's coming! We'll have to *run!* Remember, stay in bed tomorrow and I'll fix the rest. . . ."

She and Patsy glided noiselessly through the bushes and reached the sidewalk without mishap.

Peter ran to them. "It was Henry," he whispered excitedly. "Dickie is distracting his attention to give you time to get away. Oh, there he is now!"

"That was some job," panted Dickie proudly as he joined the others and walked home with them.

Joan wouldn't tell anyone about her plan, but as soon as she was home she searched high and low for the doctor's set. At last she found it in Angela's room, buried under a lot of toys.

"Here, this is what I want," she cried triumphantly, waving the scarlet fever card. "If it worked once, why shouldn't it work twice?" The others saw the idea and clapped their hands.

"But where are you going to hang it?" asked Patsy.

"On the front door," said Joan. "We'll do it after school and we'll wait till she has seen it and then we'll take it away." Patsy began to giggle, and the others joined in. They laughed for some time.

"Don't tell Mother, though," warned Joan. "She wouldn't allow it."

"Oh no, we won't," Patsy and the boys promised.

The next day, after school, the Mitchell children rushed to the White Elephant. With beating hearts they sneaked up the steps and pinned the card on the front door. Then they hid behind a maple tree. First the waiting was dull. They started to run around the tree, chasing each other. Then they got a fright, because the *Evening Star* boy mounted the steps to deliver the paper. But he paid no attention to the sign and went on his way, whistling. From sheer relief Peter and Patsy became frivo-

lous and started to fight, but Joan quieted them with a loud hiss.

"Here she comes!" They all ducked out of sight behind a parked car.

Miss Merryvale trotted up the steps of the White Elephant carrying a brief case. When she came to the door she stood still, studying the card. They could see her start and drop the brief case. Then they saw her open the door carefully and go inside.

"Now wait," whispered Joan, holding Patsy, who wanted to fetch the card back. "She'll come out again with her suitcase, just as she did with us."

The children waited for what they thought a long time, but Joan was right. Miss Merryvale appeared with the suitcase in her hand. She went to the sidewalk and summoned a taxi. They heard her say: "To the Wardman Park Hotel."

The door slammed and the taxi drove off. Joan, Peter and Patsy left their hiding place and danced around. Then they ran up the steps and took the scarlet fever card down.

"Now hush, not a word to Mother," cautioned Joan.

That evening, when Mother was putting Angela to bed, the telephone rang. Mother went down to answer it.

"Hullo," she said.

"Hullo," came a voice at the other end. "This is Mrs. Trotter."

"Oh," said Mother. "How are you?"

"Very well, thank you," said Mrs. Trotter. "What I want to know is, didn't you have a Miss Merryvale staying with you for a little while?"

"Yes," said Mother.

"Well, had you any reason to . . . er . . . think her a little strange? Did she leave you all of a sudden?"

"Yes, said Mother, "but . . ."

"She did the same to me," Mrs. Trotter interrupted in an indignant voice. "She didn't even warn me; just packed her things and went. Now she has phoned to say we have scarlet fever when we have no such thing. Una has a little cold, that's all. But she wouldn't listen to me. She kept talking about her trunk. I told her she could have her trunk and welcome, I don't want it! Scarlet fever, indeed, the *idea!* And she seemed such a quiet, sensible person. I don't know what got into her."

"I . . ." began Mother, but it was hard to interrupt Mrs. Trotter who continued.

"She probably got scared because *you* have scarlet fever and now . . ."

"But we *haven't!*" shouted Mother.

"Eh? What's that? Your children have scarlet fever, haven't they?" Mrs. Trotter asked in a surprised voice.

"No, they haven't. They just had colds," Mother told her firmly.

"My goodness! Isn't that strange! She certainly made me believe you had it. Hanna said all along it must be a mistake. She has a lot of sense, Hanna. I should have realized that you were not the kind of person to do such a thing. I am very embarrassed. My goodness, who would have thought it of that nice Miss Merryvale . . . ?"

"It was a mistake . . ." began Mother, but Mrs. Trotter went on hurriedly.

"Of course, it was a mistake. I shouldn't have listened to her. Scarlet fever! The *idea!* Do come and visit us again, Mrs. Mitchell, and bring your lovely children. . . ."

"We'll be delighted—" began Mother, but Mrs. Trotter had already hung up the telephone. Mother went upstairs, thoughtfully rubbing her nose.

"Joan," she said, "where's that doctor's set of yours?"

"The doctor's set?" asked Joan, trying to look innocent.

"Do you still have the card with 'scarlet fever' on it?" asked Mother.

"Er . . ." Joan looked uneasy. "Ye . . . es," she admitted. "Hmm." Mother fixed a piercing eye on her. "What did you do with it, lady? Own up. Did you give it to Una?"

"Oh no," Joan shook her head.

"Well, what *did* you do?" she asked. "Miss Merryvale has left the White Elephant believing that there is scarlet fever in the house. It is just a little too much of a coincidence."

"How do you know?" asked Joan.

"Let me ask you the same question. How did *you* know?" asked Mother. "If you hadn't known already you wouldn't be looking at me so calmly now." Joan hung her head and confessed what the club had done that afternoon.

"It's really very naughty of you," said Mother. "Think of the expense and bother to poor Miss Merryvale, who now again has to look for a room. It is troublesome for Mrs. Trotter, too. You'll have to apologize to her."

"But she doesn't know . . . ," began Joan, paling at the vision of such an ordeal.

"Oh, she will have to know. I can't let her go on thinking that Miss Merryvale is strange."

Joan understood and her knees turned to water. "Please, Mother," she pleaded.

But there was no help for it. When Mother got that flinty look on her face you might as well give in right away: it saved wear and tear. Seeing the terror in Joan's eyes, Mother relented a little.

"I'll go with you and explain," she promised. "All you'll have to do is to say you're sorry." Then, with a little pat on Joan's shoulder, "Cheer up. Mrs. Trotter isn't a dragon!"

TWELVE

Angela's Birthday

JOAN thought apologizing worse than going to the dentist. If only Patsy could have gone instead. Patsy never had trouble with those things; she said "I'm sorry" as sweetly and easily as she said "good night." It must be wonderful to be able to ignore your feelings, thought Joan.

Yet she knew she'd have to go through the ordeal, so she only hoped it would be over soon. It seemed as if the world had never looked so bright as that day, when Joan could not enjoy its beauty. All through her lessons she kept remembering Mrs. Trotter's face and wondering how it would look when Mother told of Joan's enormous offense. The more Joan thought about it, the worse it seemed.

But as often happens, when the dreaded moment finally arrived it wasn't bad at all. Mrs. Trotter was very cordial when Mother and Joan called on her a little after six. Mother explained the trick Joan had played on Miss Merryvale, and Mrs. Trotter didn't even frown once; she looked amused instead.

"Just the sort of thing Henry would have done," she said.

"Yes, but it was very naughty of her," Mother insisted gravely. "She realizes that. Joan, what were you to tell Mrs. Trotter?"

"I'm sorry," mumbled Joan hastily, looking the other way.

But Mrs. Trotter laughed. "We've all been young once," she said, and she and Mother began to talk of other things, leaving Joan to puzzle silently over the strange ways of grownups. Suddenly she pricked up her ears as she heard Mother invite Henry and Una to come to Angela's birthday party next Saturday.

"Why ask Henry?" thought Joan in despair, wringing her hands in her lap. "He'll spoil everything!"

But when she was outside again with Mother, nothing mattered but the feeling that the dark cloud had been lifted from her day, leaving peace and happiness, while Angela's fourth birthday shone like a star in the distance.

Birthdays in the Mitchell household followed a certain ritual. In the morning the whole family prowled about except the birthday child, who was supposed to stay in his room until everything was ready. When he was at last allowed to come down, he found the others gathered in the dining room, holding presents and singing "Happy birthday to you." This was what Angela called "the first birthday." The "second birthday" came at four o'clock, when guests arrived bearing gifts and the cake was cut.

Angela felt very excited about her birthday and told everybody what she wanted to get. Quite contrary to custom, she woke first on Saturday morning and ran around shouting: "It's my *birthday!* Get up everybody! It's my *birthday!*" Her relations awoke dutifully, and Peter pointed to the pink sky, glorious with the rising sun.

"Look!" he cried. "Look, Angela! Isn't it pretty? That's God's present for you. Look now, Angela, don't disappoint Him!"

"Oh, thank you, God," said Angela, with her best company smile, but her real interest was reserved for more tangible gifts.

She thought the family was very slow getting ready, and after a while she tried to sneak downstairs. But Mother had wisely planted Peter at the foot of the stairs, and he told her gruffly to go on up again. As she did, she collided headlong with Mr. Spencer, who was coming down.

"Oh, Angela," he said, ignorant of family customs. "Many happy returns of the day and here is a present for you." Angela drew back, her sense of decorum outraged.

"No, not *here*," she said. "You must go down and sing first." Mr. Spencer, taken aback, obediently carried his present to the dining room where he stationed himself behind the others. Then Angela was called and she came in, smiling as the familiar "Happy birthday to you!" resounded through the room.

Now the true rapture began. First came the children's presents, which indeed could not be avoided, they were thrust upon Angela with such energy. A ball was pushed against her nose by Peter while Patsy pressed a little baby bottle in her hand and Joan hung a small pocketbook around her wrist. Timmy had to wait. He was swinging in his little hammock inside the play-pen and was trying to open the paper parcel he was holding.

Mother now gave Angela *the* present, a new doll, a big rag doll she had made herself, almost as tall as Angela with yellow woolen ringlets. Angela embraced it passionately.

"Surshy!" she cried. "This is Surshy!"

"Now where does she get *that* name?" asked Grannie, who held out her present, a book called *The House at Pooh Corner.*

"Oh," said Angela, taking it. "I know that book, it's about William Pooh and Christmas Robert."

"Don't forget *me*," said Mr. Spencer, standing wistfully in the background with his scorned gift.

This time, however, Angela accepted it gratefully. "Oh, thank you enough," she said with ladylike calm. Then she saw what it was and became a whirlwind of joy. "Candy!" she shrieked. "A whole box! All for me! Real candy!"

"Gimme some, gimme some!" cried the other children, gathering around her.

Even Timmy cried, "Some! Some!" in a absent-minded way. Hidden in his hammock he had finally succeeded in opening his parcel and had found a bar of chocolate. Now he was triumphantly consuming it and soon all that was left of his present to Angela was a crumpled piece of paper on the floor and brown marks on his hands and cheeks. But Angela never noticed. She was too busy feeding Surshy her breakfast.

"Why do you call her Surshy?" asked Mother.

"Oh, *you* know, from the book," explained Angela. "Surshy said, Surshy said."

"She means: 'I'm going a milking, sir, she said,' " cried Joan, and they all laughed except Angela, who didn't think it funny at all.

As soon as breakfast was over Mr. Spencer left for his office as usual, first bowing deeply to Timmy, whom he had christened "Mr. Gandhi" because he was often dressed in a similar fashion.

"Come back early, Mr. Spencer. We're going to have a cake and Una Wendell is coming," cried Joan.

Mr. Spencer looked surprised. "Una Wendell?" he said slowly. "Who is she?"

"The girl we told you about, at the White Elephant," Patsy reminded him. "Do you know a girl of that name?"

she went on, seeing the thoughtful look on Mr. Spencer's face.

Mr. Spencer roused himself with a start. "Wendell? No, I don't know anyone called Wendell," he said. "And I'm very sorry but I can't come to your party; I have an engagement for dinner. Have a good time though!" And he waved at the children.

"Oh, Mother, what a pity Mr. Spencer won't be here," cried Joan, disappointed.

Mr. Spencer was already a full-fledged member of the Mitchell household. The children couldn't even imagine his not being there. Quite apart from his laudable habit of bringing home candy every Saturday evening, he was a person to be liked for his own sake, full of quiet humor and understanding.

"Mother," asked Joan, "can't we ask Una to come and have lunch with us? It's so long to wait until four o'clock."

"You'll have to ask Henry, too, then," said Mother.

"Oh, he won't come," Joan assured her confidently.

She had already decided that Henry was much too snooty to want to go to a party for a little four-year-old girl. She called to Peter and Patsy, but when the three of them had started on their way to the White Elephant, Angela ran after them, clamoring to be taken. It was her birthday and it would be too much trouble to bring her back, so they said "all right." Angela skipped happily at their side, clasping Surshy.

If Mrs. Trotter felt alarmed at seeing four children on her doorstep at nine o'clock in the morning, she hid it very well.

"Come in. Isn't that nice of you to visit me! Henry isn't up yet, but Una is eating her breakfast," she said. "Is this the birthday child? Congratulations, Sister."

"I'm not a sister, I'm a mother," said Angela sedately, as the children filed into the dining room where Una was sitting behind a huge plate of steaming oatmeal liberally sprinkled with sugar. Apparently she hadn't even started yet and Mrs. Trotter told her sternly to do so at once, though Una looked at her pleadingly, her first joy at seeing her friends fading from her face.

"No nonsense now," said Mrs. Trotter. "You should eat more. The doctor says you aren't gaining enough. He isn't pleased about you. You're not to get up from the table until you've cleaned your plate."

Angela looked with amazement at someone who wouldn't eat. Angela thought eating the most interesting occupation in the world.

"I'm hungry," she said loudly to whom it might concern. "I'd like some."

"Oh, Angela," cried Joan, blushing with shame. "You just had a big breakfast."

"I only had peas," announced Angela in an injured voice.

"Peas?" Una laid down her spoon and smiled.

"Oh, Angela," scolded Joan, embarrassed. "You didn't have peas."

"I did too," Angela maintained firmly.

"You did not. We don't have peas for breakfast," protested Peter. "Only for lunch and supper."

"We have too," said Angela. "Kris Peas."

"Oh, Krispies."

The children burst into laughter and Angela was offended. She wouldn't be coaxed into good humor again until Mrs. Trotter gave her a thick slice of bread and jam. Sitting down on a chair beside Una, with Surshy on her lap, she settled down to enjoy herself. Now and then she also received a spoonful of oatmeal from Una, when Mrs. Trotter wasn't looking.

"Mrs. Trotter, may Una come to lunch with us, please?" asked Joan. "And Henry," she added hastily. But Mrs. Trotter explained that Henry had to go on a hiking trip and would be away all day.

"It isn't that he wouldn't like to come, dear," she explained, to soften the blow for Joan. "Only he has looked forward so long to this outing. They are going to camp overnight."

"I understand," Joan told her quickly, much relieved. She had been worrying what on earth she would *do* with Henry, should he condescend to come after all.

"I'm ready, Mrs. Trotter," cried Una, pushing away her plate. But Mrs. Trotter lifted the spoon and uncovered a little mound of oatmeal hidden underneath.

"No, you're not," she said and Una had to take up her spoon again.

At last she was permitted to go, with instructions on how to behave, a coat in case it got cold, galoshes in case it got wet, and the injunction that she must eat all she got for lunch.

THIRTEEN

Blinkie

UNA could scarcely believe that she was really and truly going to the Mitchell home. She had heard so much about it from the children and Miss Merryvale that she'd been longing to go there for some time, but something always happened to prevent it. She wanted to see the screened porch, which Joan had fixed up for Blinkie and Bertha, the bunny. She wanted to see the fishes and Joan's and Patsy's room and the victory garden. But most of all she wanted to meet Grannie. Grannie sounded like the grandmothers she had read about in her book. Una walked so fast that the Mitchell children could hardly keep up with her.

The first one at home to greet Una was Timmy. He was holding on to the chicken wire of his fence and flattening his nose against it to see.

"Hi," he said.

"Hi!" answered Una, looking wide-eyed at Timmy's yard. "Do you keep him in a concentration camp?" she asked. Joan laughed.

"Mother!" she shouted, running into the house. "Una calls Timmy's yard a concentration camp!" Mother smiled.

"How are you, Una?" she said, drawing the girl toward her and giving her a kiss. "I'm happy to see you. I hope you'll have a good time."

"I know I will," nodded Una, her cheeks flushed with pleasure. "Where is 'Grannie'?" Mother smiled again.

"You know all about us, don't you?" she said. "Grannie is upstairs, she'd like to meet you very much." Grannie *did* like to meet Una.

"So you're the little girl I've heard so much about," she said when Joan introduced her. "*My*, but aren't you pretty. I love that shade of red hair. I was so sorry my own children turned out dark."

Una looked gratefully at Grannie. At the school she attended before she came to Washington the children had called her "carrot top."

"I like your hair too," she said shyly, gazing at the snowy masses twined around Grannie's head. Grannie really did look like a fairy-tale person, she decided. She had wide, starry eyes that made you think she knew many stories.

"Would you consider a change?" asked Grannie. "You give me your hair and I'll give you mine."

The Mitchell children and Una laughed merrily at the idea of Grannie with red curls and Una with white, but then they decided to go and see the rest of the house. Una was shown everything, from the torn wallpaper in Timmy's room to the missing tiles in the bathroom. Bertha and Blinkie were visited for a moment, and then Una had to shout through the house telephone while Joan stood downstairs at the kitchen end and shouted back.

"Come on down, all of you!" she cried. "Cora is finishing the cake."

They trooped downstairs and Una shook hands with Cora, who cast pitying eyes on the frail child. But the children's attention was fixed on the cake, a beautiful one with pink roses, yellow birds and green leaves, and "Angela" written in red letters. Cora was very proud of it and the children thanked her for taking so much trouble, while Patsy suddenly decided:

"When I grow up I'll be a maid, because I want everybody to love me."

Cora thought this a very humorous remark, and she laughed heartily at it.

"You'd better make up your mind then to do some work too," she advised Patsy.

After the cake had been admired, Una was pulled off to see other things. In fact, she was left little peace; the moment something caught her fancy and she settled down to study it, something else was sure to be shoved under her nose with the words: "Look! That's mine."

At lunch she kept gazing around in amazement. So much talking at once, so much "pass me this" and "pass me that." Such piles of biscuits and waffles vanishing in a few minutes, so many glasses of milk, or cocoa, spilt or exchanged.

Una had sat at long tables with far more people and less noise, for those people had been weary and frightened and food was a rare and sacred thing to them. Una now found the behavior of the rowdy young Mitchells so interesting that she ate her plate empty without noticing it.

Joan saw that Una admired and envied the easy freedom of her home, and she wanted to show off a little. She
scarcely listened when Mother asked her to be quiet
while Grannie took her nap, and went tearing off at the
first opportunity, uttering a warwhoop. She led the others
into the yard where they started to play "kick the can"
and "cops and robbers" with appropriate noises. They
climbed the mulberry tree and danced on the porch roof
until Cora chased them away and then they swung so high
in the hammock, five at a time, that the cord broke and
they all tumbled on the floor with loud shrieks.

Una was as wild as the rest. At first she had been timid,
but when Joan kept assuring her that "Mother and
Grannie wouldn't mind," she let loose with a bang. As
long as she could remember she had been obliged to be
quiet and well mannered for fear she'd be sent away if she
wasn't. There never had been anyone on whose love she
could count enough to allow her to be wild sometimes.
Now, in the safety of a crowd, her long pent-up energy
found a sudden release and she joined the fun whole-
heartedly, her blue eyes blazing and her red curls stream-
ing behind her. She yelled and shouted and never for a
minute wished she were anyone but Una Wendell.

Grannie gave up trying to rest and came down just in
time to receive Angela's other visitors who had come a
little early and stood on the doorstep with brushed hair,
washed faces and presents in their hands. Laura Jone's gift
was a box of handkerchiefs and Dickie's a box of crayons.
Angela greeted them merrily and guided them to the
dining room to see the cake, which now stood proudly in
the middle of the table, bearing four pink candles. The
table was laid beautifully with paper plates and colorful
"poppers," which couldn't pop on account of the war but

held paper caps inside. The children put those on right
away, after Mother had assembled them all and had
herded them into the dining room. She and Cora carried
in dishes of strawberry sherbet and then the window
shades were let down and the candles on the cake lit.

Angela sat in blissful silence while the others sang
"Happy Birthday to you," letting the sound roll over her
in a golden wave. When it was finished Angela, steadied
by Mother, cut the cake. Suddenly Una broke the rever-
ential silence by saying in her clear voice:

"Oh I *do* wish I had a birthday too, sometimes."

The children looked at her in amazement. One's birthday was the foundation of one's life, so to speak. Every
self-respecting child had one. Sometimes parents might
not go so far as to give a party, but the birthday was there
just the same.

"You *must* have a birthday, *everyone* has," said Joan.

Una shook her head. "I don't have a real one," she said.
"Sometimes I have a make-believe one, but it isn't the
same. Nobody knows the right day for it, I don't even
know exactly how old I am." The children looked at her
in dismay. Not to have a birthday was a poverty indeed

and it brought home to them as nothing else could the horrors of war. But Angela, less impressed than the others, cheerfully attacked her cake and after a slight lull the party resumed its gaiety.

When the last crumb of cake had disappeared, the children played games. They started with charades, but Joan's side changed the word in the middle, and that wasn't fair. Then Peter and Dickie had to act a pretend fight and it developed into a real one, the boys rolling over and over the living room carpet until Mother separated them and told them to play something quiet. But the children were too excited. The extra energy supplied by the cake and sherbet proved fatal. There wasn't a game in the world that could have kept them still. They were soon racing up and down the stairs, playing hide and seek and making so much noise that Mother and Grannie put their fingers in their ears while Cora murmured "Land's sakes!" over and over in the kitchen.

Presently they trooped shrieking into the screened porch where they scared Bertha and Blinkie. Blinkie especially, being more highly strung than placid Bertha, got into a panic and fled into the bedroom, under the bed. The children pursued him, yelling and laughing. Joan poked at him and the little creature, usually so trustful, darted off behind the bookcase and jumped on the folding screen. He perched there, looking down nervously, jerking his tail and muttering "chit . . . chit . . . chit." Then he leaped from the screen to the chest of drawers, got entangled in Mother's necklace, slipped on the polished mahogany, knocked down the comb and hairbrush, and tumbled to the floor. Then he quickly rushed up the curtains, Mother's necklace still dangling on his tail. Now the chase was wild indeed, all the children dancing

around and sprawling over the floor, trying to grab poor Blinkie, who was frantic. At last Angela caught hold of the necklace and Joan captured Blinkie. She thrust him back into the porch and quickly shut the door, but not quickly enough. As the door closed she felt something stick and she heard a squeal that made her shiver. It was Blinkie, who had tried to get out again and had been caught between the doors. He limped around for a moment and then lay quite still. Joan knelt down, trembling with grief and remorse.

There was a sudden, awed silence as the children gathered around her and watched, their high spirits flown, their hearts heavy. As soon as Joan touched Blinkie he squealed again, a high, pitiful squeal. Patsy and Una both burst into tears, but Joan didn't cry though her heart hammered in her throat. A minute ago Blinkie had been so alive, so soft and furry, full of movement and grace; she had felt so proud of him. Only one moment, a thoughtless drag at the door, and there he lay, smitten. If only Joan could push away that moment, wipe it out—if only it hadn't ever been. It seemed so unfair that only a *little moment* . . . but she mustn't think of that now. Blinkie needed her. She picked him up and he nestled in her arms, forgiving her for injuring him, only knowing that she was all he had to seek comfort or help from.

Mother and Grannie, more alarmed at the sudden stillness than at all the noise, came to see what had happened. Joan showed them her squirrel, which moaned a little as she moved it.

"Oh how terrible . . ." said Mother compassionately.

"But be careful, dear," advised Grannie. "Sick animals sometimes bite."

"Oh no, he won't bite me," said Joan. "He knows I am his mother"; but her lips trembled.

She had not been a very good mother, she feared. She put Blinkie on Mother's bed, and the poor little fellow tried hard to run on three legs but the wounded one dragged and hurt him. He fell over and yelped piteously. Joan gathered him to her.

"It's so hard to be a mother to a squirrel when you aren't a squirrel yourself," she said. "You don't know what to *do*."

"Call up Mr. Hollis," Mother advised.

"All right."

Joan put Blinkie back on Mother's bed, asking her to watch him, and ran downstairs. She could still hear Blinkie's yelp and the sound went like a needle into her heart. It felt just like the time she had to have stitches in her arm. Joan called the zoo, but was told that Mr. Hollis wasn't in.

"What shall I do now, Mother?" she cried, wiping her eyes with the back of her hand.

"Try a vet," said Mother. "Wait, I'll help you." She came down and rang up the number of a veterinarian who treated all animals. He was reassuring. "It is very hard to break a squirrel's front leg, almost impossible," he said. "It's probably just bruised. You'll have to watch and see. In the meantime give him a little tea, that's good for him, but no aspirin. Squirrels are allergic to aspirin. There is nothing you can do for him except to let nature work undisturbed."

That gave hope and Joan went upstairs feeling the lump in her throat melt down a little. All the same, her baby was suffering through her fault and couldn't be relieved. He was still lying on Mother's bed. He wouldn't let Grannie come near him, he tried to bite her, but Joan's touch he endured patiently. He even seemed to enjoy it when she held him in the hollow of her neck, under her chin, to keep him warm. Patsy and Una still sobbed. Joan told them it wasn't necessary.

"The doctor thinks he'll get better," she explained. "It's very hard to break a squirrel's leg."

"Oh, isn't it merciful?" sighed Patsy gratefully. Una only murmured: "I *am* glad," but she gave Joan a look which said far more.

Meanwhile the fun had oozed out of the party. Dickie and Laura's parents came to call for them and a little later Mrs. Trotter arrived for Una. Una hated to leave and only went after repeated farewells and a special hug for Joan.

That night, when all the Mitchells were at last tucked safely in their beds, Mother heard a sound as of a child sobbing. It seemed to come from the girls' room and she hurried upstairs.

It was Joan; her whole bed seemed to shake with her grief.

"What is it, Joanie?" asked Mother, patting her eldest daughter on the back.

"Oh, Mother," sobbed Joan. "I've been so bad and I meant to be so good."

"What have you done, honey?" asked Mother softly.

"Oh, *you* know," said Joan, "I just didn't care *what* I did, I tore your best dress when I hid in the closet. . . ." She watched Mother's face anxiously, but though Mother looked concerned, she didn't seem crushed. Joan took a deep breath and continued: "I also knocked down your hat and afterward people trod on it and now it doesn't look so nice any more."

"No, I don't imagine it does," said Mother resignedly.

"Well, and then . . . I ate the icing off the piece of Angela's cake you had put aside for Mr. Spencer."

"That was mean!" cried Mother quickly.

"I know." Tears dripped down Joan's nose. "But the worst is Blinkie. I shouldn't have let them all play with him and frighten him. You never let anyone touch *your* babies. Blinkie isn't a toy!"

"I'm glad you see that," said Mother. "You must learn not to forget others in your excitement." And Mother stroked Joan's hair. But Joan groaned and hid her head in her pillow.

"It had to happen just when Una was here. What must she think of me?" She wept. "Oh I wish I could begin life all over again."

Mother laughed. "Dear me," she said. "You've only just started. If you feel like that now, how must Grannie feel at her age?"

"Oh," said Joan, sitting up again and wiping her eyes.

"I bet Grannie hasn't done as many bad things in her seventy years as I in my ten."

"Come," said Mother, ruffling Joan's hair. "It isn't as terrible as all that."

"And Una *does* like you," Patsy piped up suddenly from her bed, startling Mother, who imagined her asleep. "She told me herself that you were the wonderfulest friend she had in all the world."

"Really?" asked Joan, brightening up. "Oh boy."

"There now," said Mother. "That's a nice thought for you to dream on." And after patting Joan's head once more, she left the room and went softly downstairs.

FOURTEEN

The Nursery School

BLINKIE was very much the center of the Mitchell household the next few days. The first thing Mr. Spencer said in the morning was:

"How is Blinkie?" Everyone inquired after him, even the mailman. Patsy, however, devoted herself exclusively to the fishes because she feared they were a little jealous, poor dears.

For seven days Blinkie still limped, flopping piteously about on the floor of the porch. To Peter's distress he couldn't say grace any more. Blinkie always used to say grace before meals, putting his two forepaws together and lifting up his face. But now he could not raise his right paw, though he tried hard.

After a week, however, Blinkie was able to romp about again, chasing Bertha and climbing up the screen wire as if he had never been hurt. He had an endearing way of sitting on Joan's shoulder, eating nuts, or climbing all over her and landing in her pocket, where he'd curl up and go to sleep. Bertha wasn't half so much fun, though she could eat in an interesting way, sawing off great chunks of cabbage with industrious, sharp teeth.

Una often came to visit her pet, that is, whenever Mrs. Trotter would let her. If Una had had her choice she would have spent twenty-four hours of every day with the Mitchells. But Mrs. Trotter said people shouldn't "outstay their welcome"; Mrs. Mitchell had five children already, and enough to do, not to have a sixth child bothering her all the time. Una assured Mrs. Trotter that the Mitchells didn't mind, that they all *loved* her. But Mrs. Trotter shook her head in a skeptical way and kept a restraining hand on Una's visits.

It was true that the Mitchell family had grown very fond of Una, especially Grannie. Grannie's heart was so filled with pity for the suffering war victims that she was only too happy to have one near to cherish. She loved to have Una come to her room. She kept a box of sweets carefully hidden from her grandchildren, reserving it especially for Una. While Una munched some of those, sitting on a cushion beside Grannie's chair, Grannie would tell her lovely stories of fairies and goblins, while her knotty old fingers gently slid in and out of Una's red curls. Una's love for Grannie almost amounted to a passion and was only equaled by her love for Joan.

Mr. Spencer heard a lot about Una and was longing to meet her, but somehow it never came about. He left early and came home late every day, except on Sunday. On that day he taught Sunday School and was often invited out by friends afterward.

For Una it was lovely to have the Mitchells to escape to. Henry now had his own friends, boys from his school, and when they visited him he didn't want Una around. He had started a club of his own called "The Spyshooters Union," which was supposed to hunt spies. Henry and his friends looked for enemies everywhere and delighted in pouncing on poor Una, taking her captive and questioning her out of her wits. There was now a standing feud between the young Mitchells and Henry, and consequently between the Spyshooter Union and the Five for Victory Club. Henry's club had the advantage of his beautiful yard and the clubhouse while the Victory Club was still homeless.

Fall had really set in now. The leaves on the maple trees were shivering on their stems and daring each other in sharp whispers to let go. As the first, venturous ones came fluttering down, Angela ran into the house telling Mother to "Come, quickly! the leaves are acting queer!" Last fall was so long ago she had forgotten that trees undress before they go to sleep under a blanket of snow.

Mother's victory garden was running to its end. The corn was nothing but shriveled stumps and the tomatoes a yellowing wilderness with a red fruit still shining through here and there like a jewel. If they took care not to disturb those, Mother said she saw no reason why they shouldn't build themselves a clubhouse in the backyard with some odds and ends of lumber in the basement.

Joan thought it an excellent idea. She and Patsy and Peter dragged the pieces of lumber and some empty orange crates outside and started building right away.

It was more fun to make a house than to find one all

ready. Dickie Carter had a big brother who helped them in his spare moments and lent them some tools. Una tried to help too, but she wasn't very good at carpentry. One advantage about building the hut in the victory garden was that Angela and Timmy were kept from bothering them by the fence.

The hut soon began to look like something. First the children built one little room with an old glass door fastened to it with hinges, serving as window and a door at the same time. It was much smaller than the playhouse at the White Elephant's and Henry pointed this out with glee when he came to watch over the fence.

"You wait," Joan shouted back. "We're not finished yet. And anyway, we *made* ours; you only *found* yours." All the same, the taunt rankled and presently a second story was added to the hut.

"If only we had our flag back," sighed Joan. "It would look beautiful, waving from the top!" But the flag had vanished completely, though the children had asked Una to look for it and had themselves searched the White Elephant grounds often enough.

As fall progressed from gently drifting leaves to a thick, rustling carpet on the sidewalk, and Hallowe'en came and went, with its costumes, nuts and roasted apples, Joan's hut acquired more and more rooms. At last the Spy-shooters ceased to sneer and grew jealous. Poor Una had a hard time with them, since they vented their anger on her, and she often sneaked off to Joan. Only with Joan did she feel safe.

"Henry's club is silly," Joan said. "Our club is real, we help win the war. But they don't catch real spies."

This remark was overheard by the indignant Spy-shooters, who often prowled around the Mitchells' yard now, watching the progress of the hut. They decided they would take revenge. The Mitchells' hut stood near the hedge which divided the Mitchells' yard from that of the neighbors. The Spyshooters therefore planned to enter the neighbor's yard and crouch behind the hedge. In that way they managed to witness one of the secret meetings of the Five for Victory Club.

This meeting was especially important because Joan had discovered a new way of helping her country.

"Many mothers have no maids now," she explained, after the usual blows of her hammer. "It is hard for them to get away to do their shopping when they have small children. So I think we ought to start a nursery school on Saturdays."

"How?" asked Peter.

"We could use Timmy's yard and play games with them. And we could educate them too. I've got a very interesting book. It says a lot about discipline. I don't think Mother has ever read it," Joan added reflectively.

"Why don't you lend her the book then?" asked Peter.

"Because I'd *hate* to," said Joan immediately. "I don't want her to educate us out of a *book!* I want her to use her own ideas. Does everybody agree that we must start a nursery school?"

"Yes, yes," cried the members.

"All right. Resolution carried," said Joan, noting it down in her book. But a hissing voice behind the hut made her look up.

"What's that?" she cried, running outside. The Spyshooters, seeing they were discovered, scampered off with suppressed giggles.

"My *goodness!* They spied on us, they ought to be called 'Spysnoopers,' cried Joan furiously.

"Do you think they heard of our plan?" asked Patsy anxiously.

"Oh, we hadn't discussed that properly yet anyway," said Joan. "Let's go and see the mothers now."

Four mothers in the neighborhood whom Joan approached seemed pleased with the plan. Joan would be given charge of their children on Saturday afternoon for the payment of a war stamp. There was two-year-old Andy, three-year-old Virginia, four-year-old Stephen and five-year-old Sharon. With Angela and Timmy that made six.

The next Saturday was warm and sunny, one of those fall days that are justly famous in Washington. Joan and Patsy went to fetch the children after lunch, taking Timmy and Angela with them. Meanwhile Peter and Dickie were to clean out the yard. The first child the girls went to fetch was Andy McCarthy, who now lived in the "haunted house." His sister Cathy was rocking herself on the porch.

"You'd better mind him," she told Joan. "He is a terror."

"Oh," said Joan, "he isn't half as bad as Timmy. Look, Timmy is much fatter." Timmy and Andy were put side by side. They regarded each other solemnly, their thumbs in their mouths.

"He is not," said Cathy, sitting up straight in her chair. "Andy is *much* the bigger!" Joan conceded that Andy was a little taller. "But then, he is older," she remarked. "I bet Timmy could beat him up anyway."

"He could do no such thing," cried Cathy, getting up from her chair in indignation. "Andy is the *best* scratcher! He could scratch the nose off your face!"

"And Timmy could pull your hair out by the handful!" cried Joan, not to be outdone. "And he can spit too and throw as far as that gate!"

"And Andy can kick and bite and pinch; he is a tough guy!"

"So is Timmy a tough guy!"

The girls glared at each other, while the two tough guys swayed unsteadily on two very fat pairs of legs, and eyed each other with understanding and affection. Let their sisters quarrel, they meant to have fun together. Cathy's mother came out on the porch and Joan consented graciously to take Andy anyway.

She and Patsy now collected Virginia, Stephen and Sharon without further difficulty. They returned to Timmy's yard, which had been put into tip-top condition by the boys. Una had arrived too, having escaped the clutches of the Spyshooters, who, she said, were after her. "Never mind," said Joan. "You're safe now. Come along, we've got to train these kids."

This wasn't as simple as it sounded, however. Virginia

and Sharon got into a fight and had to be forcibly separated. Andy wanted to eat a beetle and Timmy tried to take his clothes off, while Angela had to be told not to run away all the time. Joan decided that it would be easy enough to train people if you didn't have to keep them from doing what they shouldn't all the time. But "the kids" had a lot of fun. Peter and Dickie amused them by performing tricks: hanging by their knees from a tree, jumping off the porch railing, and even getting up without touching the grass with their hands. Presently Patsy said she would tell a story and the children sat around her on the grass while she told a harrowing tale of giants and thunderstorms. It was only half finished when Joan cried suddenly: "Where are Timmy and Andy?"

Yes, where were Timmy and Andy? The story hadn't interested them much and they had wandered off to the sand pile. Now Joan noticed a tiny gap between the chicken wire of the fence and the ground. Timmy and Andy must have burrowed through there like rabbits.

"Mother!" cried Joan, running into the house. "Have you got Timmy and Andy here?"

"No," said Mother. "I thought you were watching them."

"I thought so too," said Joan ruefully, "now I don't see them anywhere."

"My goodness!" Mother was out into the yard in a twinkling, calling for Timmy. He was nowhere to be seen.

"I'll go back into the house and telephone Andy's mother; perhaps he has walked home, taking Timmy with him," cried Mother. But Andy's mother hadn't seen the little boys either. She was very upset when Mother told her what had happened.

"Cathy and I will be out looking for them too," she promised.

Joan felt terrible. She was responsible for those children and now this had happened no one would trust her again. She told Una and Patsy to take Virginia, Sharon and Stephen back to their mothers and then she went to search for the little boys.

"I can't understand it," she thought. "I really *did* look after them and the yard is supposed to be safe. I inspected the fence this very morning. Darling Timmy . . . he was just beginning to talk . . ." Joan was weeping quietly and bumped into Cathy McCarthy without seeing her.

"I told you you should mind Andy," said Cathy reproachfully. "You wouldn't believe he was bad and now look what has happened."

"I guess he and Timmy are both terrors," admitted Joan, wiping her eyes. "But Timmy is such a *darling* too!"

"And our Andy then," said Cathy, suppressing a sob. "I suppose you don't think he is cute?"

"He is all right," said Joan, "but when Timmy says 'gimme googy . . .' "

"Oh, you should hear Andy say 'all gone!' " cried Cathy. "And when he has been in his bath he looks like an angel with his wet curls. What have you done to him?" And she burst into tears. Joan was ready to follow suit, but instead she grabbed Cathy by the arm and whispered:

"What's that? Did you hear something?"

Cathy stopped crying and listened.

"Yes . . ." she said. "I think it's Andy, calling 'Catty! Catty!' "

"No, it's Timmy, calling Jojo!" shouted Joan excitedly. "And it's coming from the White Elephant. I bet it's those boys; they're doing something to our babies!" Joan dragged Cathy along and ran across the street.

Presently she crashed through the hedge and into

Henry's yard, Cathy at her heels. They soon found
Timmy and Andy, each tied to a tree, big tears glistening
on their cheeks.

"Oh, my angel!" cried Joan, running to Timmy.

"My pet!" cried Cathy, running to Andy.

The babies were soon freed, but Joan was so indignant
when she saw the red marks the ropes had left on
Timmy's wrists that she told Cathy to take him home. She
was going to have it out with the boys.

"The big bullies!" she said. "Wait till I lay my hands on
them!" She prowled through the White Elephant's yard
and peeped into the playhouse. She saw no boys, but she
did see something which made her even angrier than she
was already. The missing flag, for which Joan and the
others had searched in vain, hung on the wall of Henry's
playhouse. She recognized it right away by the V on its
stick.

But when Joan entered the hut to get it the door suddenly slammed shut behind her and there was a sound of boys' laughter.

"Ha! Ha! You're our prisoner!" cried Henry. "I knew the flag would do the trick! We caught the worst traitor of all." Joan blushed. She had fallen into a trap.

"Open the door!" she cried, banging on it. "You can't go around kidnaping people! You stole Timmy and Andy too, and Mother will get the police, see if she won't!"

"She can't," said Henry, but his voice was less certain and Joan knew she had scored a point.

"Of course she can; it's against the law to take children away," she went on.

"We were just keeping them safe," argued Henry in a sugary voice.

"Nice and safe," cried Joan furiously, "with the whole neighborhood looking for them!"

"If it hadn't been for us they might have been run over," said Henry, sounding tremendously virtuous. "We didn't invite them to come here, did we, guys? They just walked here of themselves to spy on us."

"Yes! Yes!" cried the other boys, who seemed to obey Henry like little soldiers. Joan didn't know whether to believe them or not. She was sure they had stolen the children out of the yard, but she couldn't prove it. Timmy *did* escape sometimes.

"Why didn't you tell us you'd found them then?" she asked. "You might have known we'd be anxious!"

"Why should we?" More of Henry's teasing laughter. "*You* were getting paid for minding them, not *we!*" Joan heard the other boys snicker at this and she felt so angry, she could burst.

"Let me out!" she cried, kicking the door, but the boys only jeered.

"You can stay here," they shouted. "We've a nice strong bolt on it. That will teach you not to come spying here!" And they whispered and snickered some more. Then they went off. Joan could hear their footsteps dying away in the distance. She listened for a while until she was quite sure they had all gone and then she looked around for a way to escape. The window was barred with chicken wire which should not be too difficult to dislodge if she could find a sharp instrument. She rummaged in Henry's tool chest and found a shiny new penknife. Opening the blade, Joan began to pry loose the staples which held the chicken wire to the window frame. She soon had a big opening, but then she hit a stubborn staple which wouldn't come out. As she tried to force it the blade of the knife snapped in two.

"Golly," said Joan, looking at it guiltily. Then she hastily shut the broken blade and threw the knife back into the chest.

"It's his own fault," she thought, "for locking me in." And, grabbing the flag, she climbed through the hole in the window.

Mother sat with Timmy in her arms when Joan came home. She wanted to know exactly how Joan had found the little boys and she was annoyed with Henry.

"Of course, if they walked into his yard, there isn't much we can do about it," she decided. "We can only watch Timmy more closely in the future. But those boys are too wild for my taste. Some day they'll come to grief with their teasing. You keep out of their way, Joan, hear?"

"Yes, Mother," said Joan.

FIFTEEN

The Fifth Pet

WHEN Henry discovered that Joan had escaped from the playhouse he was very disappointed. He had looked forward to keeping her in suspense for a while. But he didn't find out about his broken knife until much later, when he fetched it to hollow out one of the pumpkins left over from Thanksgiving dinner. It was a terrible blow, good knives were hard to get, and this one had been a honey. He wondered who could have done it.

"I bet it's Joan," he said aloud, twirling his broken knife in his hands and scowling. "She did it on purpose because I locked her up. But I'll get even with her! I'll burn her hut down, that's what I'll do. And if she says anything about it, I'll knock her teeth out!" He was trembling with rage and shouted the last words, frightening Una. She sat on a limb of a nearby tree, reading her beloved fairy book, which Mrs. Trotter had given back to her.

"Whose teeth are you going to knock out?" she asked timidly. Henry hadn't known she was there and he jumped.

"It's none of your business," he growled, but Una was alarmed. She had feared at first that he was threatening her, but since he apparently wasn't, she wondered whom it could be. It might be Joan. Ever since Joan had stood up to Henry about that book, Henry had hated her and Una had loved her. Forgetting her fear of Henry, Una lowered herself out of the tree and repeated:

"Whose teeth?"

"What business is it of yours?" asked Henry fretfully. Then his anger got the better of him and he cried:

"Well, if you *must* know, it's that precious friend of yours, that Joan Mitchell. She broke my knife but I'll pay her back. She'll wish she never touched the thing. I'll rub her with poison ivy, that's what I'll do. A pretty sight she'll look, all swollen up. Or better still, I'll steal that pet of hers, that squirrel. *Then* won't she be sorry!"

Una's eyes opened wide with horror.

"Oh no, you musn't," she cried quickly. "Joan didn't break your knife, I did!" She had flapped out the words without thinking in her eagerness to help Joan. Now, finding Henry's eyes fixed on her in sudden blazing indignation, she trembled at her boldness.

"You did, did you?" cried Henry. "You mean little refugee, you! How *dare* you touch my things; wait till Mother hears of this!" And without giving her another glance he ran off to the house.

Una showered her book with tears. She was sure Mrs.

Trotter would be very angry. Una had been told from the very first that she must not touch Henry's things. Perhaps her punishment would be that she could not go to the Mitchells any more, or perhaps she would lose her book again. If only Mrs. Trotter didn't send her away, far from the Mitchells. That would be too terrible. And yet Una was not sorry she had taken the blame for that knife. No, she was not sorry. At least she had saved Joan, and no matter what happened, she would stick by what she had said.

It was a determined-looking Una who walked a little later into the White Elephant's parlor, to face Mrs. Trotter. But Mrs. Trotter wasn't angry, only very sad.

"Is it true that you broke Henry's knife?" she asked.

"Yes," said Una.

It was hard for her to say the word, her lips felt so stiff, but out it came, ending in a sharp hiss which seemed to drop into a well of silence. Mrs. Trotter took hold of Una's thin, cold little hand. Her eyes were full of tears.

"I wanted so much to make you happy, Una," she said. "Why couldn't you have been a good girl? Then this wouldn't have happened. Henry is so angry now, he says he'll run away if you stay here. This is his home, Una, I can't do that to him. I'm very, very sorry, but you'll *have* to go." Una's fortitude deserted her at this blow. Her worst fears were realized and she began to weep quietly, like a grown person. Mrs. Trotter felt very sorry for her.

"Don't take it so hard," she said. "I'll see to it that you find a good home."

"When must I go?" sobbed Una.

"Oh, we won't hurry things," said Mrs. Trotter soothingly. "Poor child, you look worn out. You'd better go upstairs and lie down awhile." With a kind pat on Una's cheek Mrs. Trotter pushed the child out of the room.

Alone on her bed Una lay rigid with grief. As far back almost as she could remember she had been shoved around from place to place like a bad penny. No sooner had she become fond of someone when she was moved on again. There seemed to be no resting place anywhere in her turbulent little life, except for a golden spot at the very beginning of her memory. Then she had been loved and cherished by three people, Mummie, Dadda and Gwamp. She could still see their faces as in a rosy haze, and she remembered sitting on Gwamp's knee and reading with him out of her precious book. It was one of the reasons why the book was so dear to her. But bombs and flames had made an end of that early paradise and real life as Una knew it now meant depending on strangers for food and affection, with the possibility of being sent away the moment you began to feel at ease. It was confusing and unsettling and Una knew she couldn't have borne it but for the little Heaven locked in her breast, the faces of Dadda, Mummie and Gwamp. It now seemed as if those three were close beside her, consoling her, and worn out with weeping Una laid her head on the pillow and fell asleep.

When she awoke it was dark. Una wondered what had happened. She had slept so deeply she did not immediately recollect her troubles. She rubbed her eyes and yawned. Suddenly she clutched her bedpost and sat still, frozen with horror. On the window sill, against the black sky, sat a spook with a luminous face. It stared at her with a leery grin and fiery eyes. Una screamed, a piercing scream which cut through the house like a whiplash. The next minute she had fallen on the floor in a dead faint.

When she came to, the room was light, she was lying on her bed and Mrs. Trotter and Hanna were bending over her anxiously. The glowing image was gone; only an old, cut-up pumpkin stood on the table.

"There, honey," said Hanna soothingly, bathing Una's face with eau de cologne. "You're all right now."

"It was only a faint," she told Mrs. Trotter in an aside. "She got scared by the pumpkin, that's what it was. Henry ought to be whipped for putting it there."

"He didn't mean it so badly," Mrs. Trotter said quickly to defend her son. "Many's the time we used to play that trick on each other when we were youngsters and none of us ever fainted."

"Likely none of you'd been through a bombing," remarked Hanna dryly. "It seems to me this child is feverish. I'd call a doctor if I were you."

"Do you think so, Hanna?" asked Mrs. Trotter nervously. "I'll call the doctor right away." And she left the room. Una was glad that Hanna stayed, Hanna was so kind. Her old hands soothed Una's forehead until the child dropped off to sleep again.

The doctor was not pleased with Una's condition.

"She has had a bad scare," he told Mrs. Trotter. "It has upset her emotionally, which may do a lot of mischief to her state of health. Better keep her in bed for a week or so and give her plenty of strengthening food. I'll prescribe a tonic."

"I don't understand . . ." faltered Mrs. Trotter. "It was only a harmless little joke."

"My dear madam," said the doctor, "you have no idea how often I am called in to repair the damage caused by harmless little jokes." And with this cryptic remark the doctor departed, leaving Mrs. Trotter more puzzled than ever.

Of course the story of Una's illness soon reached the Mitchell household.

"Dickie says that Hanna told him that Henry scared Una with a pumpkin!" cried Peter as he came home for lunch the next day. "And she fainted and the doctor had to come and now she is sick."

"Oh, the poor child," said Mother.

"Dickie also said that Hanna told him that Una is going away," Peter went on dramatically. He was not disappointed at the effect his words produced. A bomb could not have caused more consternation.

"Going away?" cried Joan. "Where?"

"Anywhere," said Peter. "Mrs. Trotter isn't going to keep her."

"That poor lassie!" cried Grannie. "Couldn't we take her, Rita?"

"I'd love to," said Mother. "But honestly, I don't see how we could afford it and, after all, is it fair to John? He has so many dependents already."

"No, of course, you're right," said Grannie. "It would be most unfair to John. We must not let our hearts run away with our heads. But I never felt so sorry for a child as I feel for little Una."

"Why doesn't Mrs. Trotter want to keep Una?" asked Joan, suspecting that Peter had not told all yet.

"Because she broke Henry's knife!" ended Peter with a whoop. "And you know very well you did that, Joan. You told me so yourself. So it's all your fault."

"Is that true?" cried Joan, her eyes blazing. "Then I'm going straight to Mrs. Trotter." And flinging her napkin down she left her lunch on her plate and rushed out of the house, not heeding Mother's and Grannie's cries of protest. Across the street she ran, straight into the White Elephant's yard and up its front steps. She pushed the bell hard and Hannna came rushing to open the door.

"Can't you be a little quieter?" she scolded when she saw it was Joan. "That poor child is sleeping. I guess you wanted to see her?"

"No, I want to see Mrs. Trotter," said Joan firmly.

"Oh." Hanna looked surprised. "Mrs. Trotter isn't in," she said. "She is at her work now. She'll be in at six." That was a blow. Joan hated to see her determination wasted on a futile mission. Later she might lose courage.

"Can't I leave a message?" she asked.

"Yes indeedy, come in." Hanna opened the door of the parlor and gave her a pencil and some paper.

"Dear Mrs. Trotter," wrote Joan. "I broke Henry's knife myself by accident. I guess Una wanted to take the blame because she is my bosom friend. I hope you'll let her stay now." Here a tear splashed on the paper and smudged a word but Joan went on. "I'll give Henry another knife. Please forgive Una. Yours respectively, Joan Mitchell." She folded the paper and wrote "Mrs. Trotter" on it.

"Don't give it to Henry," she told Hanna anxiously.

"No, of course not," promised Hanna. Joan remembered that she had to go to school and left in a hurry, wondering where she was going to get a knife to give back to Henry.

But when Mr. Spencer came home that night and heard what had happened, he offered to give Joan his own knife, a good prewar one with three blades. Joan thanked him fervently and immediately ran to the White Elephant to give it to Mrs. Trotter for Henry. Mrs. Trotter was ever so kind. She thought Henry would be very pleased with the knife. He had gone to a party but she'd give it to him when he came back. She thought it sweet of Joan to confess what she had done and she heaped candy in Joan's lap, but nothing could change her mind about Una.

"It can't be helped," she explained sadly. "It doesn't work out with Una here. It is better to face it right away than to ask for more trouble later. Henry is my first duty, and since he feels as he does, there is no way out."

Joan's heart ached for Una, but there was nothing she could say, so she left. Just as she set foot on the sidewalk the sirens blew the first warning for blackout practice.

"Golly," thought Joan, "I don't want to be caught outside!" And she ran home as fast as she could, just reaching the front porch when the second warning wavered through the street. All the lights in the house were out, of course, and Joan groped her way to Grannie's room where the Mitchells always sat during blackouts. It had heavy drapes which made it possible to keep a small light beside Grannie's bed. The rest of the family was gathered already around the open fire, which, with its cheery flames, dispelled some of the gloom. Even Timmy was sitting on the bed, sucking his thumb. They were all glad to see Joan safely back.

"I just made it," she confessed. "Ouch! does my side ache! I never ran so fast!"

"Well, and what did Mrs. Trotter say?" asked Grannie. "Is Una going to be allowed to stay?"

"No," said Joan gloomily. "Henry doesn't like her and Mrs. Trotter says her first duty is to him."

"Well, I suppose she is right," said Mother. "But I'm terribly sorry."

"I've an idea it might be the best thing in the world for Henry to learn to put up with Una," remarked Grannie.

"But it might not work out so well for Una. She is too sensitive to be exposed to Henry's jokes."

"I wish I could meet the child once," complained Mr. Spencer. "If you don't take care she'll have left without my ever setting eyes on her and I confess that I am interested. Judging from your stories she must be a little like my granddaughter . . . poor little Eunice. . . ." And Mr. Spencer looked dreamily into the fire.

"Tell us about Eunice," pleaded Patsy. It was not often they had Mr. Spencer at their mercy for questioning. Usually he was too busy, but now the blackout kept him from reading or writing. He was holding Angela on his lap. She had fallen asleep and her golden curls lay scattered over Mr. Spencer's coat sleeve.

"Eunice?" he said now, smiling gently. "I'll be glad to talk of her. I can't ever think of her as dead, she was so intensely alive. Not that she was in any way extraordinary, she was just a normal child, I suppose, but she seemed pretty wonderful to us. I lived with my daughter after the death of my wife, so I knew Eunice from the day she was born. We used to be great friends. We'd go for walks together and I'd teach her the alphabet. Angela here reminds me a little of her though Eunice's curls were fatter and had a coppery sheen to them. She didn't talk as well as Angela, though; she always wanted me to 'wead' to her. I said 'weeding you do in the garden.' Then she made me go with the book to the garden to 'wead' to her. She loved fairy tales and she could recite them from her book as though she could read. She knew her letters, of course, but I think she did most of it by memory. That was bright though, for a child of five, wasn't it, Mrs. Mitchell?"

"I should say it was," said Mother.

"Yes, she had great promise," sighed Mr. Spencer,

stroking his forehead as if to smooth his wrinkled thoughts. "It was a great pity . . . a great pity."

At that moment the doorbell rang.

"Oh dear," said Grannie. "I hope there's no light showing."

"I'll go down," said Mr. Spencer, but Mother was already groping her way downstairs. It was strange, she thought, how difficult it was to keep light from showing through those drapes. She opened the door.

"I'm sorry," she began. Then she let out a yell, for a man had thrown his arms around her and was embracing her.

"Don't you know your own brother?" he cried.

"Jim!" Mother shouted with joy. "Grannie! Children! Uncle Jim has come!" The dark hall was suddenly in a turmoil. The children flung themselves downstairs in such a hurry that it was a miracle they arrived unhurt. Grannie came too, clinging anxiously to the banisters. Uncle Jim embraced everyone, though he could not possibly know which was which. Suddenly a hoarse voice remarked:

"Hi ya, fellows. Ain't this a terrible war?"

"Goodness, who is there?" cried Grannie, startled. She was holding on to Uncle Jim so she knew it couldn't be he, and anyway Uncle Jim had a musical, manly voice and not a husky croak.

"Did you bring a friend?" asked Mother. Uncle Jim laughed.

"Sure," he said. "Mr. Jenkins. Would you like to meet him?"

"But *Jim!*" cried Mother. "Why don't you introduce him? That's a terrible way to treat your friends." Uncle Jim only laughed the more.

Mother groped around in the dark. There didn't seem to be anyone there.

"Don't fret, everything will be OK," said the hoarse voice again, now somewhere just behind her.

"My goodness!" cried Mother. "Where are you, Mr. Jenkins?"

"Mr. Jenkins! Mr. Jenkins!" shouted the children, dancing around the dark hall. Uncle Jim laughed so, the house seemed to vibrate with the warm ruggedness of his voice. At that moment the "all clear" sounded and Mother switched on the light. There was no one in the hall except Mother, Grannie, the children, and Uncle Jim, who looked very tall and handsome and weatherbeaten in his uniform.

"Where is Mr. Jenkins?" asked Mother, amazed.

"Hi ya, fellows," came the croaky voice again. "Ain't this a terrible war?" And Uncle Jim uncovered a cage which was standing beside his suitcase. In it was a big, gray parrot.

"Hullo," it said. "Meet Mr. Jenkins."

And that's how the Mitchell household acquired its fifth pet.

SIXTEEN

Out with Uncle Jim

JOAN wondered why it was that uncles and fathers were so noticeable when they were home and mothers and grannies when they were away. Perhaps it was because uncles and fathers were more exciting and mothers and grannies more necessary.

Uncle Jim certainly was a wonderful person, and it was a delight to have him back again. The house rang with his laughter and high spirits; cigarette smoke spiraled up to the ceilings and Mother's rugs served again for ashtrays, since Uncle Jim had many more exciting things to think of than where the ashes went to. All of life was a party to him. He carried celebrations around like the lady with rings on her fingers and bells on her toes. As Peter said,

Uncle Jim was better than a birthday. Perhaps it was because no comfort seemed too humble for him to enjoy. He loved Grannie's open fire and played with it like a child, throwing on bits of paper and kindling to make it flame up and quarreling with Grannie about the best way to keep it going. He loved good food and a glass of beer and he must have read all the books in the world, thought Joan, for he could recite so many poems and sentences by heart. He had a flute, too, on which he played a little, and after dinner he would ask Grannie to sit at the piano and then they would all stand around and sing "Drink to me only with thine eyes," his favorite song.

Uncle Jim was interested in everything. He made jokes with Cora in the kitchen, he taught Grannie a new game of solitaire and learnt one from her. He made paper airplanes for Peter immensely superior to those Peter made himself. He inspected Joan's hut and pronounced it unsafe, working a whole morning to fortify it. He replaced all the severed arms and legs of Angela's rubber doll, which was a test of will as well as muscle. He romped with Timmy, talked politics with Mr. Spencer, read fairy tales with Patsy, and praised the children to their mother until there wasn't a nook or cranny of the house which hadn't basked in the rays of his presence. But sometimes Uncle Jim would snatch his cap and go out on an errand of his own. Then the Mitchell household would relax into its humdrum grooves, the day having lost its glamour.

One evening the whole family was gathered around Grannie's fire, listening to Uncle Jim's tales of the war.

"I'm glad I'm in the naval air force," he was saying. "It may not be the most exciting job to patrol the seas in a Catalina and battle submarines, but at least you're not injuring civilians. And my crew is a wonderful bunch of fellows. I'm proud to be their pilot, and I'd hate to let them down more than anything. I guess sharing danger together makes you feel that way." Uncle Jim smoked and looked into the fire.

"I wish you wouldn't have to go back to the war any more," cried Patsy, climbing on Uncle Jim's knees and flinging her arms around him. "I don't want anything to happen to you."

"Yes, but you wouldn't want me to be useless, would you?" asked Uncle Jim. "You don't keep your dolls in a drawer because you're afraid they'd get broken if you played with them? They'd be no use to you there and I'd be no use here, with Mother and Grannie."

"Oh yes, you would," said Patsy. "You could help Cora peel potatoes and you could make beds and . . . and repair electricity, and . . ." She stopped, for she noticed that Uncle Jim didn't look very happy at the idea. Even to Patsy it seemed a pity to waste Uncle Jim's splendor on beds and potatoes, so she gave up with a sigh.

"Well, anyway, we can keep Mr. Jenkins," she murmured, to console herself. Mr. Jenkins was already a popular member of the household. Uncle Jim had bought him from a sailor who had wanted a change of conversation. Now the parrot hung in the dining room and entertained the Mitchells instead. Joan was especially delighted with him, though she *did* wonder what Daddy would say of her steadily increasing menagerie.

The children hadn't seen anything of Una since Uncle Jim had arrived. They supposed she was still in bed. They would have visited her if it hadn't been for Uncle Jim, but his leave lasted only ten days and they didn't want to miss a second of it. He would not be able to celebrate Christ-

mas at home, but he promised to take the children into
the city to see Santa Claus before he left.

Angela said she had never seen Santa Claus.

"But you are too small; Uncle Jim could not possibly
take you," protested Mother.

"Sure I can, let her come along," offered Uncle Jim
generously.

"But Jim!" cried Mother. "You don't know what you are
undertaking! You'll have a terrible time of it."

"Oh, leave it to me," said Uncle Jim grandly. "If I can
pilot a plane I guess I can pilot a bunch of kids." Mother
wasn't so sure, but she was so happy for Angela that she
let it be.

It was a cold, crisp clear morning in December when
Uncle Jim sallied forth with his little crew. The children
felt proud to walk with an officer-uncle. He was so handsome in his uniform that people turned to stare after him.
Uncle Jim was proud of the children, too. He hoped everyone would think he was their father, but since they
"Uncle Jimmed" him every two seconds it was unlikely.
Some day he really ought to have kids of his own, he
thought. The trouble was that they had to have a mother
and Uncle Jim hadn't met her yet.

The bus was almost empty when Uncle Jim shooed his
nieces and nephew inside and paid the fare. The older
children all went to kneel on the back seat to look out of
the window, but Angela sat down beside Uncle Jim. The
sun was in her eyes and she pointed at the shade.

"Pull the skirt down," she commanded. The bus
started and Angela sat quietly, looking around her.

The older children were playing a game.

"Let's pretend we're in Heaven," said Joan, "and

everything is made of something to eat. I bet that car is made out of chocolate."

"And the street of hard candy," said Patsy.

"And the clouds out of that fluffy stuff you get at the circus," invented Joan.

"And the sky of lemonade!" cried Peter.

"But then it would rain," said Joan. "And what would it be at night?"

"Cocoa," said Peter promptly.

The bus was filling up rapidly; all the seats were now taken. Uncle Jim rose to offer his place to an old lady. Peter immediately followed his example and gave his to a young lady, a pretty yeoman of the WAVES. Patsy wanted to offer her seat to a young man, but Joan told her in a loud whisper not to do that.

"Ladies only get up for old people or for sick people," she said. Patsy looked the young man over carefully but he seemed in splendid health. Luckily an old lady came along and Patsy jumped up with a whoop of delight.

"Here, look, you can sit here!" she shouted, almost pushing the lady off her balance. Then she and Peter practiced how long they could stand without support, falling repeatedly against Uncle Jim. Joan also found someone to give her place to and now only Angela was seated, feeling rather out of it. A lady with a baby in her arms entered at the next stop, looking with despair at the occupied seats, so Angela gladly offered hers and promptly fell into the lap of the WAVE lady as the bus lurched forward again.

"You can stay here, honey," said the WAVE lady. Angela looked her over and liked her. She had twinkling gray eyes, dimples in her cheeks and golden brown hair which curled prettily under her cap.

"Thank you," said Angela, trying to make herself comfortable on the rather narrow lap of the WAVE lady.

"You don't have much to sit on," she remarked. Several people laughed, but Uncle Jim looked steadily out of the window.

"What's your name?" asked Angela, conversationally.

"Mary Sullivan," said the WAVE lady.

"Oh, mine is Angela. I think my name is prettier. And I have a li'l baby at home called Timmy."

"Goodness," said Yeoman Sullivan, properly impressed. Meanwhile Peter and Patsy had got into an argument, making a great deal of noise.

"She is a WAC."

"No, she is a WAVE."

"She's got a cap like a WAC's."

"I tell you, I *know* she is a WAVE." The whole bus was giggling by now and Uncle Jim blushed.

"Hush, you two," he said, "or I'll send you straight home."

"But isn't she a WAVE, Uncle Jim?"

"Isn't she a WAC, Uncle Jim?"

"Who?" asked Uncle Jim, taking care to look everywhere except at Mary Sullivan.

"Her, of course," said Peter impatiently. "The pretty lady who is holding Angela. Look at her, Uncle Jim, isn't she nice?" Uncle Jim was blushing more than ever. With a hasty glance at the lady in question he mumbled:

"Sure . . . sure. Won't it be nice to meet Santa Claus?" But Peter wasn't thinking about Santa Claus. He thought he had never seen such a beautiful lady.

"You're a WAVE, aren't you?" he asked of her, moving a little closer. She nodded, her dimple showing.

"See?" cried Peter triumphantly. "See, Patsy, I was right, she says so herself!"

"Hush," said Mary Sullivan. "You must not talk so loud, your uncle doesn't like it." Peter looked at Uncle Jim, who certainly had an unhappy expression on his face.

"My uncle is a bashfuller," he said. "Are you a bashfuller?"

"First tell me what a 'bashfuller' is," said Yeoman Sullivan.

"Oh, you know," explained Peter. "Someone who isn't married."

"Yes," said Mary Sullivan. "Then I'm a bashfuller, too."

"I know a riddle," said Peter. "Five times eight is forty and seven times six is forty, too. Is that right?"

"No," said Yeoman Sullivan. "That's wrong."

"Caught!" crowed Peter. "Seven times six is forty-*two*, isn't it?"

"Oh, I see," Mary Sullivan smiled. "That's a good one."

"Do you know who Mr. Jenkins is?" Peter continued. "Mr. Jenkins is a parrot. Uncle Jim gave him to us. He is neat. You must come and see him, will you?"

"I'd love to," said Yeoman Sullivan politely.

Uncle Jim spent most of the bus trip admiring a colorful advertisement for lemons and he felt relieved when at last he could steer his unruly crew out of the bus. Peter lingered to say good-by to Mary Sullivan, but Uncle Jim didn't look around *once*.

"We'd better take care we don't get run over," he said, when the five of them stood on the sidewalk again. "Let's hold hands and play 'follow the leader.' I'm the leader," he added significantly.

The children liked the idea and, holding hands, they spread out in a long row. First they went lengthwise and that was all right, but then Joan got the idea of stretching across the sidewalk and intercepting other pedestrians. The children enjoyed this a lot but the pedestrians didn't, so Uncle Jim decided to break up the formation.

"Joan, you take Angela and walk in front of me," he commanded. "Patsy and Peter will each hold my hand." That way it worked better.

"You wanted to see the White House, Patsy, so we'll walk past it," Uncle Jim announced. "We can't walk close to it because it's wartime, but we can walk on the opposite side of the road. Look, there it is."

The children gazed respectfully in the direction Uncle Jim pointed, but Peter seemed worried.

"Isn't it a bit small, though?" he asked in a troubled voice.

"Small?" asked Uncle Jim. "No, it's quite spacious."

"I don't think you could lie down in it," observed Peter. "Is the man standing in front the President?" Uncle Jim looked mystified until he realized that Peter had mistaken the white sentry box for the White House, and then he roared with laughter. He pointed out the palace which really housed the President and Peter sighed with relief. The sentry box had seemed such a pathetic home for the nation's Commander-in-Chief.

Now Angela clamored to be taken to the "Caterpillar," and it was some time before Uncle Jim discovered that she meant the Capitol. He explained that there would be no time for it if they were to visit Santa Claus, and he quickly hustled the children into a department store. It was full of Christmas shoppers and beautifully decorated.

"Santa is on the fourth floor," said Uncle Jim. "We'll go up the electric stairway. You follow me." Lifting Angela on his shoulder he mounted the stairs. At the third floor he looked back, but to his surprise he saw no Peter, Patsy or Joan. He hated to be conspicuous and called softly:

"Children!" but there was no answer. Then Angela screamed:

"Peter! Joan!"

"Hi!" came a voice from the bottom of the stairs.

"*Will* you come up!" thundered Uncle Jim, throwing all modesty to the winds.

"Sure," answered Joan in a calm, reasonable voice, and after a while the three culprits emerged, panting noisily, their cheeks red with exertion.

"We were trying to go down, Uncle Jim!" cried Patsy. "It was such fun! Now I know why Alice and the Red Queen had to run so fast to stay in the same place, they were on an electric stairs!"

"Well, you'd better stay with me now," grumbled Uncle Jim. "Whew! What a crew!"

Without further mishaps they arrived on the fourth floor, a kind of toy paradise. Angela wanted to see Santa Claus right away, but Uncle Jim said he had some shopping to do first.

Mother had given Joan and Patsy and Peter a quarter each to spend, but it was not easy to find something at that price. At last Peter decided to keep his quarter while Patsy and Joan pooled their money to buy a sewing kit.

Meanwhile Uncle Jim had made his choice, too, telling the salesgirl to send it to a certain address.

"And now we'll visit Santa Claus," he promised, to Angela's joy.

Santa Claus sat in a little house without doors. A long line of children and mothers stood in front of it and the Mitchells had to take their place at the end. The line moved slowly and Uncle Jim grew tired of waiting.

"You mind the children while I get some cigarettes," he told Joan.

"All right," said Joan.

At last it was Angela's turn to go into Santa's little house and whisper something to the gentleman with the white beard.

"I want a dolly," said Angela, "and a carriage and a doggy."

"Have you been good?" asked Santa Claus.

"Sure," said Angela, and received a book. She was almost out of the little house when her conscience smote her.

"I was bad one day, though," she shouted, to the general amusement of the waiting crowd.

Now it was Peter's turn and he announced that he could sing a song. He started without further ado, in a ringing voice:

> "Santa Claus with beard so white,
> Traveling through the snowy night,
> Tall and red against the moon
> Oh please let the war end soon!"

People around stopped talking and listened.

"Fine, fine," said Santa Claus, pushing a book into Peter's hand and turning to Patsy.

"There is another verse," protested Peter, and Santa Claus had to listen again as he continued:

> "Santa, also fill the hands
> Of children in other lands.
> Heal their hearts and wipe their eyes
> And give them back their peaceful skies."

It was now quite still around Santa Claus. Everyone was listening to Peter.

"Fine, beautiful," said Santa Claus, patting Peter on the shoulder and turning to Patsy again. But Peter wasn't finished.

"There's another verse," he remarked conscientiously.

> "Though the world bends down in pain,
> Santa, give us hope again,
> Sootblack chimneys may hold stars . . .
> Santa, give us no more wars!"

There was a general applause when Peter had ended and Joan heard one lady say to another:

"What a cute little boy." She felt proud of Peter. She and Patsy now had their turn at Santa Claus and received their books. Patsy and Angela flopped on the floor, regardless of dust and feet, to admire the colored pictures at their ease, but Peter and Joan stood watching for Uncle Jim. At last he came.

"Ready?" he asked. "Fine. Come along then." Angela had got up and was dancing around, saying something which Uncle Jim didn't understand.

"What is it?" he asked. Joan whispered in his ear.

"All right," he said. "You take her. We'll wait." He lit a cigarette and leant against a counter while Joan and Angela hurried off.

"It's no use trying to get out of waiting with children," he thought. "Wait you shall and wait you must, whether it's for one thing or another." He was musing to himself and blowing out rings of smoke when Joan and Angela returned, Angela with beautiful clean hands. She insisted that Uncle Jim bend down to smell them.

"I washed my hands," she crowed. "And it had funny soap, in a bottle. And a towel came out of a li'l house and Joan threw it away." She was apparently much impressed with her experiences.

"But where are Patsy and Peter?" asked Joan.

"They're here. . . ." Uncle Jim looked around. "No, they're not. Where *are* they? Come along, we'll have to look for them." At first Uncle Jim was not alarmed. He thought that they couldn't have gone far away, and he went to what he considered the strategic places, where the most attractive toys were displayed. But when the other half of the crew remained missing he got worried.

"Where *can* they have gone to?" he muttered. Angela was beginning to complain of weariness and thirst, so he heaved her on his shoulder again and strode through the store, Joan trotting after him.

"Have you seen a little boy and a little girl in blue coats?" he asked at Information. But Information merely looked blank. Uncle Jim frowned as he stalked around, and Joan was getting out of breath. They bumped against people, hurried down aisles, and asked and asked and asked:

"Have you seen a little boy and a little girl . . . in blue coats, yes, a little boy and a little girl. . . ." Uncle Jim was getting hoarse and Joan had a terrible vision of Peter and Patsy stolen by strange men to dance and sing in a circus. Perhaps someone had heard Peter sing for Santa Claus and had waited around for a chance to pick him up. . . . Joan shuddered. How Uncle Jim felt could only be guessed from the little drops that gathered on his forehead and nose.

"By all the goblins and fairies," he muttered. "What *can* have happened to them!"

"Perhaps they are trying to go down the 'up' electric stairs again," Joan suggested. Uncle Jim quickly ran there to see, but without success. At last a fat woman, who noticed Uncle Jim's worried face and heard him call: "Peter, Patsy!" said:

"Is it a boy and a girl you're looking for, Officer?"

"Yes," cried Uncle Jim, a flash of hope brightening his blue eyes.

"They've been in the elevator these past thirty minutes," said the woman placidly, pointing her thumb at the elevator doors. "They're having a grand time."

"Grand time be blowed," growled Uncle Jim, but he heaved a sigh of relief. It wasn't long before the vagrants were hauled forth.

"We had free rides!" they cried joyously. Uncle Jim gave them a good scolding.

"In the air force you'd be court-martialed," he said.

"Now go off and wash; you look as if you'd been in a coal mine. How can I take you to a restaurant that way?"

"Oh, take us to one which shows the food, so we can choose," cried Peter, ignoring Uncle Jim's rebuke. "You always get the wrong things guessing from a card."

While they went off to wash, Uncle Jim blew Angela's nose. At last they were all ready to go in search of food. Uncle Jim brought them to a cafeteria where colorful dishes were temptingly displayed behind a glass counter.

"How much do we spend?" asked Joan.

"Take what you want," said Uncle Jim.

"You mean . . . we don't have to count, we can just take *anything*?" gasped Peter.

"Anything," smiled Uncle Jim.

"Oh boy, you must be rich," concluded Peter with a sigh of content. "Mother always gives us forty cents each." He immediately chose two hamburgers, an ice cream sundae, cake with a cherry on it and a bottle of pop. After a moment's reflection he added a slice of lemon meringue pie and carefully carried his loaded tray to the table. Joan's choice was more conventional: she watched Uncle Jim and took what he took: chops, peas, apple pie and coffee. She felt very grown up with coffee and blushed guiltily when Uncle Jim looked at her tray, but he didn't notice anything wrong.

"Want a roll?" he asked. Joan nodded and he dropped one on her tray.

Patsy consulted beauty rather than taste, and chose a glamorous salad, pink jelly with whipped cream, and a pretty cake with yellow icing. Angela only wanted ice cream and milk.

"I'm not hungry," she announced.

"Too much excitement," observed Joan, patting her curls.

"Poor Timmy, he has nothing," said Peter. "I'll save my cherry for him," and he dug into his food with so much ardor that Uncle Jim put out a restraining hand.

"You're not a dive-bomber," he said. "Go easy." Angela enjoyed her ice cream, most of which she spilt on her dress. Her glass of milk stood too close to the edge of the table and a sudden movement of her arm knocked it off and to the floor where it smashed to pieces, milk splashing all over the place. The waitress scolded her as she cleaned up the mess and Angela looked at her reproachfully.

"I'm only four," she said. "I don't know any better."

Uncle Jim quickly paid the bill and left, hiding his rather grubby charges in the merciful darkness of a movie house.

When they came out again, blinking at the light and slightly dazed after having shared the adventures of Walt Disney's Bambi, Angela lay curled in Uncle Jim's arms, fast asleep.

"Now for home," said Uncle Jim, leading a weary little crew through the streets to the bus stop. Suddenly Joan's eyes widened and she grasped her uncle's sleeve.

"Look at that little girl," she whispered. "She is crying. It's . . . it's . . . yes! It's *Una!*"

SEVENTEEN

Yeoman Sullivan

UNA had spent an unhappy week in bed. She had longed and longed for one of the Mitchell children to come and visit her, and not knowing about Uncle Jim, she hadn't understood why they didn't. It made her feel more forlorn than ever, and to make matters worse she had suffered from a toothache. Hanna had treated it with oil of cloves, aspirin and icebags, but it hadn't been of any use; the tooth kept aching.

"She'll have to go to the dentist," Hanna told Mrs. Trotter. "I guess so," said Mrs. Trotter. "I have to go to the city on Saturday anyway, to buy Henry some clothes, and I'll take her with me."

So on the same Saturday that Uncle Jim took out his crew, Mrs. Trotter and Henry brought Una to the dentist. The sore tooth was soon fixed, but Henry grumbled at the delay. He had to have new shoes and a best suit to wear at the Christmas parties he had been invited to.

"I do wish we didn't have to take Una along," he complained. "A fellow doesn't want to be gaped at by a girl when he is trying things on."

"No, of course not," said Mrs. Trotter. "I don't imagine it would entertain Una very much either. We'll take her to a movie and we'll fetch her there when we're through."

So it was arranged. Una was only too delighted to be spared the ordeal of shopping with Henry. She had seldom been to a movie and it was a big event for her. Mrs. Trotter didn't know much about the films that were going, but they passed a movie house which had *Journey for Margaret* across its front in big letters and pictures of a little girl on its bulletin board.

"I think you'll enjoy this," said Mrs. Trotter, and bought a ticket for Una.

"Take a seat near the aisle," she said, "and stay right there, even if you have to see the show twice. We'll be coming for you." She spoke a moment to the attendant at the door, who found a seat for Una.

Una was thrilled. There was a comic film on, something about a dog with a bone and another dog who wanted to steal it. Una had never laughed so much in her whole life. Then the main feature began. For a while Una was interested, though she wondered where the little girl was, but then something terrible happened. She felt herself again buried under a pile of bricks, aching all over, her eyes blinded by dust and an acrid smell of sulfurous smoke in her nostrils. She could again hear the roaring of flames, the deafening noise of explosions and crashing buildings.

Una shut her eyes, but that was no help against the sounds. Without thinking she crawled under her seat, as if to protect herself. Putting her fingers in her ears she cried "Mummy! Mummy!"

An attendant came walking toward her, but it was some time before he found her under the seat. Then he talked to her soothingly and led her to the rest room where a matron bathed her face and gave her a glass of water to drink.

"Did the movie scare you, honey?" she murmured in a comfortable, pleasant voice. "I don't blame you. I don't hold with these here war films. The world is crazy enough, I say, without rubbing it in. Your mother shouldn't have let you come here, not a scraggy, shivery child like you. You tell her that from Martha, honey."

Una let the kind words glide over her like a soothing stream, without answering. She drank the water that was offered her and gradually ceased to tremble. When she felt better she thanked the matron and walked out of the movie house. She didn't ever want to see a film again and she thought she could very well wait outside for Mrs. Trotter. So she paced up and down the sidewalk in front of the theater for what seemed to her a long time, until the cold wind froze her feet and hands. Then she decided she'd rather go and meet Mrs. Trotter. She remembered the direction in which she and Henry had gone, so she walked that way, taking great care to cross at the green lights.

After a while, however, there seemed to be so many streets, all exactly alike, which Mrs. Trotter might have taken, that Una thought she'd better go back to wait at the movie house, after all. She retraced her steps, only to find that she came out at a different place. After that she was all mixed up and didn't know the way. She was growing weary and cold, and her newly filled tooth still ached. She tried to ask someone the way, but since she didn't know the name of the movie house nor the name of the film, the gentleman couldn't help her. Una thought that probably Mrs. Trotter was already there, looking for her. She'd be angry with Una for running away. If she didn't find Mrs. Trotter, what would happen to her?

"What's the matter, little girl?" asked a friendly voice. "Did you lose someone?"

"I've lost *everyone*," said Una, looking up with tragic eyes. The lady laughed. "That sounds terrible," she said. "Perhaps I can help. You weren't out with an uncle, by any chance, were you?"

"No," said Una, "I have no uncle. I was out with Mrs. Trotter and Henry."

"And what happened?" asked the lady, who was dressed in a blue uniform.

"They had to go and shop and . . . and . . . they brought me to a movie with a little girl in it, but I didn't see a little girl, it was only bombs and I got scared. So I went away and now I don't know where I am."

"Oh, my dear," said the lady. "That *is* a mix-up. Well, let's go back and perhaps we'll find Mrs. Trotter. I think I have an idea what movie it was, I saw it myself."

So, with her hand safely in the friendly lady's, Una found her way back to the movie house, only to be told by the attendant that Mrs. Trotter and Henry had come to call for her and had left again, in great anxiety about her.

Una promptly burst into tears, and the lady tried in vain to console her.

"I don't know the way home!" sobbed poor Una, looking wildly down the street. Suddenly she let out a cry as of a liberated bird.

"There's Joan!" she shouted. "I see Joan!" and she flew to meet Uncle Jim and his crew, rushing into the arms of the oldest Mitchell child.

"Joan! Oh Joan! Take me home! I'm lost!"

"All right, honey," Joan murmured soothingly. "I and Uncle Jim'll take care of you. Don't you worry. What happened?" While Una told her adventures to the Mitchell children, Uncle Jim stared at Una's new friend, who saluted him. Uncle Jim saluted back, blue twinkles in his eyes.

"I see we are destined to meet, Yeoman Sullivan," he said. "I suppose I'll have to introduce myself. I'm Jim Mitchell." It was now Yeoman Sullivan's turn to look anywhere but at Uncle Jim.

"This little girl is lost," she said in a businesslike voice, studying the top of Una's head. "Do you know her?"

"I don't, but my niece seems to," said Uncle Jim, wasting his most charming smile on an indifferent world.

"Well, then, I don't think I'll be needed any more. I'm rather busy," said Yeoman Sullivan.

"Not too busy to drink a cup of coffee with us, I hope," pleaded Uncle Jim, wasting another smile.

"Oh, *much* too busy," said Yeoman Sullivan, saluting again and marching off, her heels clicking frostily on the pavement.

"Whew! Was that a tailspin!" said Uncle Jim, looking regretfully after Yeoman Sullivan's pretty, slim figure. He was soon recalled to real life, however, by Joan, who tugged at his sleeve and said:

"Uncle Jim, this is Una. She is lost, but I told her she can come back with us."

"Oh, of course, naturally," said Uncle Jim. "The more the merrier. How do you do, Una?"

"How do you do, sir," said Una, dropping a curtsy.

"And how did you get to be lost?" asked Uncle Jim, shifting Angela to his other arm. She was still sleeping. All the children began to tell him at once; Uncle Jim couldn't make head or tail of it.

He just said "Yes, yes," at regular intervals and watched for a bus.

When a fairly empty one stopped, he chased the children inside and followed with Angela. They all collected on the back seat. But the bus had scarcely started again when Joan discovered that she had left her and Patsy's sewing kit at the restaurant and she wanted to get out at the next stop and go back to look for it; but Uncle Jim said "no."

"No," he vowed rashly. "I'm not going to leave this bus until we come to our own stop. Here is a quarter each for you and Patsy, then you can get yourselves another kit." The girls were delighted. They had already thought of many things they'd rather buy, like the lady with three wishes. And here they had their choice all over again. Meanwhile Angela had waked up and was climbing around on the empty seats. Uncle Jim now pulled Una on his lap and tried to find out what had happened to her.

"So the movie scared you, eh?" he said. "When you've heard real bombs you don't want to listen to movie ones. Sensible girl. You and I, we're alike. We've seen action. All those civilians, they don't understand, do they?"

Una couldn't quite make out what Uncle Jim meant, but she looked at him gratefully because he was so kind.

"Now you must tell me how you came to meet that lady you were with," Uncle Jim went on. "She was a kind, pretty lady, don't you think?"

"Oh, yes," said Una "and she is terribly wise, she knew right away which movie it was."

"Dear me," said Uncle Jim, "that was clever of her. Do *you* remember the kind lady, Angela?"

"Mary Sullivan?" said Angela doubtfully.

"I like Santa Claus better."

"*I* liked the lady," cried Peter. "She is *my* friend and she is going to visit Mr. Jenkins."

"Uncle Jim," cried Joan, "please tell Una the story of when you had to hold your breath."

"Not here in the bus," said Uncle Jim.

"Why not?" asked Joan. "It's an interesting story. Other people would like to hear it too. You see," she told Una, "Uncle Jim had to go to a doctor and hold his breath before he could be a pilot. He had to hold it for . . . I think it was *sixty* seconds; that's very hard, if you don't cheat. Uncle Jim practiced and practiced but he could only do it for fifty seconds. At last he had to go to the doctor and he wanted so badly to be a pilot he thought, 'I'll hold my breath till I burst'; so he held his breath and held it and held it and he felt wobbly and queer but he thought, 'I'll get into the Air Force if I *die*,' and he held it and he held it until his breath exploded out of him. He was so afraid it hadn't been sixty seconds he sat shivering on his chair, and then the doctor laughed and laughed and said he'd held his breath longer than anyone else and made a record. Wasn't that funny?" The children chuckled and some grown-ups too, to Uncle Jim's embarrassment.

"I bet I can hold my breath for sixty seconds," said Peter, closing his eyes and opening his mouth. He sat absolutely rigid, as if his breath were a team of wild horses. He got redder and redder in the face, but at last he gave up and inhaled with a gulp.

"I did it for seventy-eight counts," he boasted. Joan now tried it, too, and Patsy and Angela and even Una, until there was a blessed quiet around Uncle Jim.

But after a while Peter turned white instead of red.

"I'm sick," he said.

"Yes, I'm sick, too," echoed Patsy.

"And *I'm* sick!" shouted Angela.

"It's the bus," Joan told Uncle Jim. "The smell makes them sick."

"Oh dear!" Uncle Jim looked horrified. "What am I to do? What does your mother usually do?"

"That depends," said Joan. "When it's bad she says: 'Bear it.' When it's worse she tries to get us near an open window, and when it's still worse she gets off the bus because she says it isn't fair to other people if . . ."

"I understand," said Uncle Jim hastily. "How bad do you think it is now?"

Joan looked appraisingly at her suffering brother and sisters. "Middling," she decided. "Let's open a window." So she and Uncle Jim opened a window and Patsy, Peter, and Angela had to stand near it. The wind was very cold and Uncle Jim wondered whether it was the right thing to do. It had begun to snow and the children's hair was soon covered with melting flakes. Anyway, it didn't help. Peter looked almost as pale as the snow and threatened that "something" was going to happen. So, in spite of his vow, Uncle Jim got off the bus ten blocks too soon.

It was a very weary, cold and hungry crew which marched into the Mitchell home that Saturday afternoon.

"My goodness," said Mother. "You *do* look tired. Did you have a good time?"

"Oh *marvelous*," said Uncle Jim, pulling a face. "My, I'll be glad when I'm back on duty and can take a rest. I take my hat off to the pilot of a home." And he gave Mother a kiss.

"Don't say I didn't warn you," chuckled Mother. "Sit down and have some food while you tell us about your trip. There's a tasty stew waiting for you on the stove."

Grannie and Mother watched the children and Uncle Jim eat while they listened to the stories.

"And what did you do with Una?" asked Mother, when she heard that the child had traveled back with Uncle Jim.

"We brought her home first, of course," said Joan. "Uncle Jim said that Mrs. Trotter would be anxious about her. She was, too; she seemed very glad to have Una back, but she would have been angry if Uncle Jim hadn't explained about the movie."

"Poor Una," murmured Grannie. "It's a shame to think of that sensitive, imaginative child adrift in the world."

"Why is she adrift?" asked Uncle Jim. "She seems to have a substantial home . . . almost a palatial one."

"Oh, she isn't remaining there. Mrs. Trotter can't keep her," said Mother.

"Poor kid," cried Uncle Jim. "Shall I adopt her?"

"Oh yes, Uncle Jim, *do!*" shouted the children, charmed with the idea.

"And leave her to John's wife to take care of, I suppose," Grannie remarked dryly. "You'd better get yourself a wife of your own first." Uncle Jim looked sheepish and changed the subject. He never once mentioned Yeoman Sullivan. Mother and Grannie heard about her from Peter, who kept talking of the "lovely lady."

"She is my friend," he explained, "and she is going to meet Mr. Jenkins. I hope she doesn't forget."

The next day, Sunday, was the last one of Uncle Jim's leave. There was a festive sadness about it, a treasuring of each moment, already flavored with the bitterness of parting.

There was to be a special afternoon service at church that day to pray for the soldiers, but the Mitchells didn't want to break up Uncle Jim's last evening, so they decided to stay home. It was to be a very special evening. Mother had prepared all Uncle Jim's favorite dishes for dinner, and Joan and Patsy had, with great pains, learned by heart his favorite poem. They were going to recite it for him as a surprise. They also planned to dress up in their best clothes. Uncle Jim would be sure never to forget his last day at home.

Only Peter insisted on going to the afternoon service. "Daddy is a soldier," he said stoutly. "He needs to be prayed for."

He arrived at church rather late and plopped down in a pew, breathless with running. A lady was kneeling beside him and Peter glanced at her. Then he had to smother a cry of surprise. The lady was his friend, Yeoman Sullivan. Peter found it hard to keep his attention on the service and as soon as it was over he spoke to her. To his disappointment, she didn't recognize him immediately.

"I'm *Peter!*" he said. "Your *friend.* I met you in the bus and you're going to see Mr. Jenkins, don't you *remember?*" Yes, with a sudden blush, Yeoman Sullivan *did* remember.

"Do come, do come *now!*" cried Peter, dragging her out of the church. "You'll only forget again if you don't." And before she knew it, Yeoman Sullivan was walking up the steps of the Mitchell house.

"Mother, Mother, here's my friend, the *Lady!*" cried Peter, overjoyed.

Mother, Grannie, Uncle Jim, Joan and Patsy were having tea in Grannie's room, around the fire. They were glad to see Yeoman Sullivan, especially Uncle Jim. He wouldn't hear of her not staying, and dragged forth a chair for her and poured tea for her and handed her a slice of cake and some buns and cookies. This time his smiles were not wasted, and as Mary Sullivan displayed her dimples, Uncle Jim's smiles grew warmer and warmer.

Mother and Grannie didn't get a chance to speak to the guest; Uncle Jim claimed her whole attention. He gaily bandied words with her, quick, sparkling words that seemed to leave a golden haze in the room. At last Uncle Jim leaned forward in his chair, his eyes alight under their long, black lashes.

"How would you like to go out with me tonight, Yeoman Sullivan?" he pleaded. "We'll have dinner somewhere and see a show!"

"I'd love it," said Yeoman Sullivan, blushing gently under the golden twinkle of her curls.

So presently she and Uncle Jim descended the front steps on their way downtown.

The deserted Mitchells watched them go from the hall window, tears in their eyes.

"What did you have to bring *her* here for, Peter?" Joan asked gloomily. "Just so she could spoil our last evening?"

But Peter was more desolate than anyone.

"She is *my* friend," he sobbed. "And she never even *looked* at Mr. Jenkins!"

EIGHTEEN

Christmas

UNCLE JIM left the next day early. Though the last evening hadn't gone exactly as the Mitchells had planned, Uncle Jim *did* say he would never forget it.

"I want to thank Peter for the most glorious evening of my life," he said, with eyes like stars.

But Peter wasn't there. He had gone off with his un-spent quarter to buy a souvenir for Uncle Jim. When he returned at last, a box of candy clasped to his breast, Uncle Jim had already left. Peter sat down on the front steps and wept bitterly. Grannie went to him.

"What a lovely present you have there," she said. "Is it for me? It is just what I wanted to cheer me up."

"Oh," said Peter, looking up. "Oh, Grannie, you may

have it. I meant it for Uncle Jim, but you may have it."
And after a while the tears dried on his cheeks.

Christmas was on the way now; you could feel the air
hushed in anticipation.

The house became a den of conspiracies. Whispered
conversations were carried on in corners, drawers hastily
opened and closed with a rustling of paper, and all members of the family wore mysterious smiles.

Mother was hard put to it to keep from guessing what
she was going to get. The children would tell her with
what letter it began, what it rhymed with, how much it
cost and where they had bought it, but Mother didn't
guess a thing.

Joan and Patsy asked her one evening, when she was
tucking them into their beds:

"Mother darling, isn't there anything you want desper-
ately? Isn't there *something*, costing about twenty-five
cents, that you have *longed* for all your life?"

Mother felt ashamed and a little sad that there wasn't.
There should have been, she thought. There should have
been some wonderful thing, costing twenty-five cents,
that would have made her supremely happy. But all she
could think of was safety pins.

Mother and Angela went to buy the Christmas tree
together. It had to be a living one, for there were to be real
candles on it. Mother didn't like electric lights.

"What's a length of glowing wire behind colored glass
compared to the wild, free, fragrant flame of a candle?"
she said. And if the tree wasn't dry and the ornaments
weren't inflammable, the danger of fire was not great.

To Joan's delight, Una would still be there for Christmas. The Refugee Committee couldn't take her back
until January. The Mitchell family spent quite a lot of

time planning surprises for her. They all wanted to give her something before she left. Unfortunately she couldn't spend Christmas with them because Mrs. Trotter had made other plans, but she was in and out of the Mitchell house as often as she could.

On Christmas Eve she helped Joan and Patsy decorate the hall and living room with boughs of balsam and holly. Peter and Angela were stringing cranberries and popcorn for the tree, and Mother was in the kitchen, preparing the Christmas dinner in advance, with Cora's help. Cora would have the day off for Christmas. There wasn't a turkey, but Mother had managed to get a goose, and the smell of its roasting mingled with the odor of eggnog and the pungent scent of balsam.

"Oh, I wish you were here tomorrow, Una," sighed Joan, as she fastened a garland of holly to the banisters. "I bet you won't have half as good a time as we!"

"I know it," murmured Una sadly. She wished with all her heart that she were Joan's sister. Sometimes she pretended she was, but a careless remark would be sure to jerk her out of dreamland. She now looked around her with homesick eyes. The rather shabby appearance of the Mitchell home was hidden by a green mantle of love. The living room seemed a veritable bower, with its tree in the middle, still untrimmed. Una heaved a deep sigh.

Suddenly the telephone rang, and Mother came from the kitchen to answer it.

"It's I, Mrs. Trotter," said a voice. "Is that Mrs. Mitchell?"

"Yes," said Mother.

"Oh, I wonder whether you can help me. . . . I'm in a terrible fix."

"What can I do?" asked Mother.

"It's Henry. He came down with measles and the doctor won't let Una come back here. He says she may get it anyway, but she is in too delicate a condition to take chances. He says he won't answer for it if I let her return. I'm at my wits end!"

"She may stay here," said Mother immediately. "My children have all had measles."

"Oh, do you mean it? Oh! that *is* a relief. I'll send Hanna over right away with her clothes. I can't tell you how grateful I am."

"You're entirely welcome," said Mother, putting down the phone. Then she smiled at the children.

"Guess what!" she cried. "Henry has the measles and Una is going to stay here for Christmas!"

Una flew at Mother and hugged her and kissed her while the other children slid down the banisters and did other acrobatic tricks to vent their joy.

"Listen, we've got work to do," Mother reminded them, taking off her apron. "I'm through with cooking, Cora can do the rest. Now we're going to trim the tree."

The children stood around as Mother opened the boxes with ornaments and took the glamorous old friends out of their tissue-paper wrappings. With so many hands to help, the little tree soon shimmered in familiar splendor, hung with colored balls, silver trumpets, icicles, tinkling bells, and angel hair. Mother put up the candles and fastened cookies and candy canes to the bowed branches while Peter and Angela added their cranberry chains.

Mother and the girls now cleared away the papers and boxes while Peter went to fetch Grannie. Grannie admired everything, saying, as usual, that this year the tree was prettier than ever. Then she went to the piano and played carols while the children sang.

A ring at the door interrupted them. It was Hanna with a suitcase.

"Here are Una's clothes," she said.

"Come in, come in," cried Mother, pulling her inside. "You have to admire our tree and our crib and you have to taste our eggnog and cake. Don't you know it's Christmas Eve?"

"Yes, Hanna, stay awhile," pleaded Una. "It's so lovely here!"

"I haven't time," grumbled Hanna, but she let Mother take off her coat all the same. "Here is your suitcase," she told Una. "Look and see if I forgot anything." Una opened her suitcase and rummaged in it.

"You packed my *book!* " she cried happily. Hanna smiled.

"I thought you'd like to have it," she said.

"Oh, Hanna, you're a darling. And what is this?" Una held up a little parcel, neatly wrapped in white paper with red ribbons around it. Hanna blushed.

"That's, er . . . just a little Christmas gift from me," she mumbled.

"Oh, let's see what it is, Una," cried Joan and Patsy. Una unwrapped the package and discovered a glass ball with a little village inside it. When you turned it upside down, it snowed on the village.

"Oh, how beautiful!" cried Una. "*Thank* you, Hanna."

"I thought you'd like it," said Hanna, flushing with pleasure. The children all had to make it snow in turns, while Mother brought Hanna a glass of eggnog and a slice of fruit cake.

"That's an unfortunate thing for Mrs. Trotter, to have Henry come down with measles just before Christmas."

"Yes, ma'am, it is," agreed Hanna. "But I'm kind of glad for Una. I know she'd rather be with you folks."

"You're fond of Una, aren't you?" said Mother.

"Well, who wouldn't be?" grumbled Hanna. "Poor little mite. But I really have to be going now. Mrs. Trotter will be wondering what's happened to me. Thank you so much for the eggnog and cake. . . ."

"Well, good-by, Hanna, and happy Christmas to you."

"Where is Una?" asked Hanna, looking around.

"Here I am!" Una had gone upstairs to fetch something which she now gave to Hanna.

"I hadn't time to wrap it," she explained. "It's a handkerchief. I made it for you. Joan showed me how."

"Thank you, honey, I'll keep that to remember you by," said Hanna, wiping her eyes with it. "Good-by now, and be a good girl!"

The children waved Hanna off from the hall window and Mother called them in to a simple supper.

That night Una hung her stocking from the living room mantelpiece beside those of the Mitchell children, and she sang with them:

> "Please remember us this year,
> We've been *angels*, Santa dear!"

Mother had put up an extra bed in Joan's and Patsy's room for Una, and the three girls soon were fast asleep, dreaming of overflowing stockings.

Mr. Spencer came home late that night. He had been shopping and was very tired. Mother told him of her unexpected guest.

"Good," said Mr. Spencer. "Then I'll meet little Una at last. But don't wake me early tomorrow, please. I'm going to sleep until it's time for church; I feel exhausted. You never saw such a crowd shopping. I honestly believe there isn't a *thing* left to buy. Don't count on me for lunch tomorrow either, but I'll be back for dinner with you.

"Try to come at four o'clock," begged Mother. "Our party really starts then. The children are going to act a play they have made up themselves. I don't know how it will turn out." And she smiled.

"I'll be there," promised Mr. Spencer.

On Christmas morning Mother woke to find the house strangely cold. She went down to investigate and saw that the furnace wasn't running. She put the automatic regulator up higher, but there was no answering hum from the basement.

"Out of oil!" said Mother. "On Christmas day! Well, whatever happens it mustn't spoil the children's fun."

So she went down to the cellar and fetched up blocks of wood which she piled beside the living room fireplace. Then she made a fire. It seemed like a spark in an icebox, but it did help when you sat close to it and it added the cheerful smell of wood smoke to the fragrance of the tree. Mother went upstairs again and almost collided with Patsy, who came tearing down the steps in all manner of excitement.

"There are pictures on our windows!" she cried. "Real Christmas pictures, all white and sparkly. Come and look, Mother!" Mother went up obediently, and was greeted by Una and Joan with "Merry Christmas" hugs and shown the windows, on which the night's frost had painted delicate ferns and flowers.

"We used to see those often when I was a girl," she said. "I used to lie awake and watch the moon shining through them. But the hot waterpipes have chased them. Our furnace isn't working today."

"Oh, isn't it *lovely?*" cried the girls. "Such a surprise for Christmas!"

Peter had now discovered the ice flowers, too; he and Angela were trying to make holes in them to look through, and their joy was great. Mother told all the children to put on warm bathrobes and slippers and then they could go down to see what Santa had brought them. They soon scrambled downstairs and found their stockings filled with tangerines, peanuts, hard candy, marbles, crayons and other small presents. Timmy only had a trumpet and some cookies, because he was still a baby.

Grannie came in, rubbing her hands.

"Merry Christmas!" she cried. "Isn't it cold, though?"

"We're out of oil," explained Mother. "And I fear there is little chance of getting any on Christmas day. But here's a comfortable seat by the fire."

"And we've presents for you, Grannie!" cried the children, who now dealt out their surprises. Mother was very pleased with a pin cushion Una had made for her and Grannie thanked Una warmly for a pot holder. Una herself got quite a lot of homemade little gifts from the Mitchell children, and so did Mother and Grannie.

"Now I've got a surprise for *you*, children," announced Grannie suddenly. "Uncle Jim has bought something for every one of you. Go and look in the hall!"

The children ran shrieking out of the room, leaving Mother and Grannie to pick up papers and prepare breakfast.

Uncle Jim had done the children proud.

"He must be *terribly* rich," said Peter. There was a speed wagon for him, with wooden wheels, a doll carriage for Angela, a pair of stilts for Joan, and a new doll for Patsy. Cries of rapture filled the hall and to top it all they found a rocking horse for Timmy. Uncle Jim had even remembered Una and had left her a book of Grimm's fairy tales. When the children's excitement died down somewhat, Mother called them back to the living room. She had put breakfast on a low table and the children were allowed to sit around the fire with their cereal on their laps. Only Timmy refused. He wouldn't come off his horse and Mother had to feed him while he rocked back and forth.

Outside, through the frosty air, bells chimed merrily, and the children had to hurry up and get dressed or they'd be late for church.

The rest of the day slipped by quietly. After a simple lunch, which they ate near the fire, Joan announced that they had to get ready for the play. She took the older children upstairs while Mother dressed Timmy in his best white suit and drew the drapes to shut out the gray light of the waning day.

"We're ready, Mother," cried Joan's excited voice from upstairs.

"Mr. Spencer hasn't come yet," said Mother. "But I'll arrange the chairs and fix your stage so you can start the minute he arrives." The stage was only the front half of the dining room with a folding screen for background. The sliding doors would serve as curtains, and Mother placed chairs in a semi-circle to seat Grannie, Mr. Spencer and herself. Then she poked up the fire and put more logs on.

"Can't we start now?" cried Joan impatiently. It was past four o'clock.

"All right," said Mother. There was some scuffling and whispering behind the closed sliding doors while Mother and Grannie seated themselves, Timmy on Mother's lap.

Mr. Spencer arrived just in time and sat down, too, wishing Mother a merry Christmas. She and the children had been at church when he had left in the morning.

Then Joan opened the doors. She was dressed in biblically draped blankets, with a teacloth over her head, a point of which kept falling into her eyes. Holding a sheet of paper in her hand she announced:

"This is a story of a family in Bethlehem. There are three children, the oldest is Ruth (that's me). The next is Esther and the little one is Rebecca. They see the star and hear that a king is born. They sneak out of the house to bring him presents and get lost. Their guardian angel saves them, though," she added hastily, for fear of burdening the audience with unnecessary suspense.

"Act one!" she cried.

This act showed Patsy, Joan and Angela looking out of an imaginary window and pointing at what they said was a star. Perhaps it was just as well that Joan had told the plot first since the acting was so realistic as to make it hard to discover what it was all about. The children shouted and jumped about, slapped each other, seemed in great fear of an imaginary parent who had threatened to spank them if they left the house, and were having a lot of trouble with their clothes, especially Rebecca, who had a tablecloth tied around her waist over which she kept tripping. At last, in the final exodus, when the children had decided to follow the star and brave their parent's wrath, Rebecca calmly stepped out of her skirt and left it sitting in the middle of the stage. Joan shut the doors, announcing that act one was over. Everybody clapped, especially Timmy.

Then the doors opened again and showed Ruth and Esther limping through what was called a wood, and telling each other in doleful tones that they couldn't see the star any more and had lost Rebecca as well. Notwithstanding these misfortunes, however, they were very kind to a poor mother and a baby with whom they shared their food.

Then the doors closed. The second act was over. Joan opened the doors again when there had been enough clapping to satisfy her.

"Now the children are very unhappy because they haven't found Baby Jesus and Rebecca is still lost," she announced. "Also, they have forgotten the way home. But the angel comes and brings Rebecca back to them and tells them they *have* seen Baby Jesus. It was the poor baby they helped."

The wailing of the children was so realistic that Mr. Spencer felt tempted to put his fingers in his ears, though he magnanimously forbore to do so. There was an amused expression on his face. But when Una came trotting on the stage, dressed in Patsy's yellow organdy frock, with tinsel in her hair and gold paper wings fastened to her shoulders, Mr. Spencer suddenly gripped the arms of his chair and grew as white as a sheet. His eyes filled with tears which overflowed and rolled down his cheeks. He opened his mouth several times but no sound would come.

Una was getting ready to say the pretty little speech Joan had taught her when she caught sight of Mr. Spencer. She stood rooted to the ground, her eyes rounder and rounder in her little face. Then she stretched out her arms and stepped forward, uncertainly at first, but faster and faster, until she leaped into Mr. Spencer's arms, saying just one word, which brought a lump into everyone's throat.

"Gwamp!!"

"Then . . . then it's true, you *are* Eunice!" cried Mr.

Spencer, clasping her against his breast. "I thought perhaps my eyes deceived me . . . I thought perhaps an extraordinary likeness . . . But oh, my darling, you haven't forgotten your old grandfather, have you? . . . Let me look at you . . . you are older, yes, but I know those eyes and that little nose . . . Only how thin you are, how thin . . . What have they done to you, my lamb?" Mr. Spencer was stroking Eunice's hair with a trembling hand and talking as if to himself. The Mitchells looked on in open-mouthed amazement.

"It's his bombed grandchild. . . . Una was Eunice all the time and we never knew," whispered Joan in Patsy's ear. Patsy nodded. She didn't want to miss a word of what Mr. Spencer was saying and a tear of sympathy rolled down her nose. The younger children kept as still as mice. They couldn't understand what had caused this sudden emotion, but they were awed by it.

Mr. Spencer was gaining control of himself. He noticed that his tenderness made Eunice shy. So he frowned at her and said gruffly:

"Don't tell me you *still* haven't learned to say the R."

Eunice blushed and hung her head. Mr. Spencer put a finger under her chin and lifted it up.

"Say grandfather," he urged.

"Grandfather," repeated Eunice meekly.

"There, thank goodness, you gave me a fright. Calling me 'Gwamp' like that!"

"I thought that was your name," murmured Eunice. Mr. Spencer kissed her.

"Of course you did, sweetheart, it was your old name for me," he whispered. "Don't you remember how you used to ask: 'Gwamp, wead to me?'" Una's eyes brightened.

"I still have the book!" she cried. "I'll show you!" And she slipped off his knees and ran upstairs. Mr. Spencer turned to Mother and Grannie.

"I know now why the name Wendell sounded so familiar," he said. "I had never thought of the possibility of Eunice surviving her parents so I didn't realize she might be the only source of information about her identity. She was probably asked her name, and then she must have answered 'Euny Wandall,' which was what she called herself. It was naturally changed by strangers to Una Wendell. She knew her letters, but I'm not sure she could spell her name."

"Here it is, Grandfather!" cried Eunice, throwing her beloved book on his lap. Mr. Spencer opened it.

"Yes," he said. "Look, this is my handwriting." And, wiping his eyes, he read:

"To my little granddaughter, Christmas 1938." The letters were blurred and the little book looked battered and ravaged. It seemed to bear the marks of the tears and kisses with which it had been cherished through all these unhappy years.

"If there were no other way of knowing, this would be proof enough that she is my grandchild," said Mr. Spencer, handing the book to Grannie. Then he took Eunice's hands in his and looked gravely into her eyes.

"Try and remember, sweetheart," he said. "Do you know anything of your father and mother?" Eunice regarded him thoughtfully.

"There was a lot of noise and flames," she said. "And I was sick. When I was better the lady said they were in Heaven."

Mr. Spencer sighed. "I feared as much," he said. "Which lady said that?"

"The fat lady who looked after me. She was always crying *Och hamel*, and put me in her car because the Germans were coming," explained Eunice simply. "She was the mother of Vim and Emmy, but they went away when we came to another place where a thin lady took care of me. She said *Mon Dioo* and *she* put me in a wagon with a lot of other people. I don't remember so well all the things that happened," sighed Eunice.

"There was a nice gentleman who called me '*sanoreeta*' and *he* put me on a ship. Do I *have* to remember everything?" Eunice looked so forlorn that Mr. Spencer smiled, pressing her to his heart.

"No, dearest," he said. "It will be my privilege to make you forget it all. The main thing is that I have you back now." He turned to Mother and Grannie. "I'm *so* glad she recognized me. It simplifies everything."

"Yes, it is a mercy," Grannie agreed.

The children were getting over their first amazement and now they all began to talk at once, jumping about in their clumsy costumes.

"You've got a home now, Una!"

"Isn't it fun, Una, to have a *real* grandfather?"

"Will you live here always now?"

"Will I?" asked Eunice, looking at her grandfather.

"For a while, anyway," smiled Mr. Spencer. "If Mrs. Mitchell can board us both.

"Indeed, I'd love it," Mother promised warmly.

Eunice was still not quite sure of her good fortune.

"Am I yours for ever and always?" she asked of her grandfather. "Do I belong to you as much as Henry belongs to Mrs. Trotter?"

"Every bit as much," Mr. Spencer assured her. Eunice gave a sigh of deep content.

"The only thing I worry about," said Joan, "is how we are going to remember calling her Eunice. We're so used to saying 'Una.' "

"I like Eunice better, though," observed Patsy. "How do you spell it?" Mr. Spencer told her, and Joan cried triumphantly:

"It starts with an 'E'! I always did say Una was an 'E' girl!"

The lovely day was coming to a close now. While the children went up to put on their party dresses, Mother and Grannie prepared the dinner and lit the tree.

By the light of the soft flickering candles the Mitchell family presently ate a delicious meal of goose, cranberry sauce, browned potatoes and peas. When the dessert arrived, the candles on the tree had burnt low and the blue flames of burning plum pudding shone eerily in the dark.

After dinner Mr. Spencer dealt out his surprises for the family, a box of candy for everyone, even for drowsy Timmy; and Grannie sat at the piano and began to play carols.

The children crowded around her, singing from full and happy hearts. Mr. Spencer had drawn Eunice close to him, and looked down on her again and again, pouring out his gratitude in song. Una looked up at him, an answering joy in her eyes. The happiness of these two seemed to spread in waves, enveloping the others in a golden flood and rippling on in ever widening rings to all the corners of the earth.

It was the loveliest Christmas the Mitchells had ever known.

NINETEEN

Eunice's Birthday

MR. SPENCER had no difficulty in proving to the Refugee Committee that Eunice was his grandchild. The book alone, with Mr. Spencer's writing in it, was enough to convince anyone. So the formalities were soon complied with and the custody of Eunice was duly transferred to Mr. Spencer.

Mrs. Trotter felt very happy when she heard that Eunice had found a grandfather. She called on Mr. Spencer and told him how much she liked Eunice and how hard it had been for her to decide to part with her. Mr. Spencer thanked her warmly for her care of his grandchild.

For Eunice, who was still often called "Una" by mistake, a new life began from the moment she and Mr. Spencer recognized each other. At first it felt strange to belong to someone again, but after a while it seemed as if she had never been away from Gramp. She remembered the wrinkles around his eyes when he laughed and the way he smoothed his forehead with his hand when he was worried.

Mr. Spencer complained that Eunice left him no freedom. She had to sit beside him at table and she had to be the one who handed him his food. She was very jealous of the other children. Mr. Spencer had to assure her all the time that he wouldn't rather have had Joan, or Patsy, or Peter; that it was Eunice he wanted most in all the world. Sometimes Mr. Spencer feared to wound the feelings of the Mitchell children.

"You must not ask such questions, it isn't nice," he'd tell Eunice, but Joan assured him that they all understood and went to some pains to demonstrate to Eunice how much more her grandfather loved her than any of the Mitchells.

"He was always talking about you," she said.

"He was so sad sometimes because he was missing you so much," helped Patsy.

"He was quite mechanical over it," cried Peter.

"Melancholy, you mean," Joan corrected him.

"Well, anyway, he *was*," said Peter hurriedly.

The only one who didn't quite understand was Angela. She had been Mr. Spencer's special pet for so long, she still insisted on some attention; but because she was such a baby Eunice didn't mind. She and Mr. Spencer would smile at each other and enjoy together the funny things Angela said.

It was a joy to the grown-ups to see the way Eunice throve in her new-found happiness. She seemed a different girl entirely. She began to put on weight, her cheeks grew round and rosy, and her legs were beginning to look like Patsy's. She would always be graceful, but she was no longer skinny. She hardly ever imagined any more that she was somebody else, either.

"I like being Eunice," she said. "I didn't like being Una." But sometimes, just for the fun of it, she played she was Una again, and crawled under tables and chairs, pretending she was being bombed. The Mitchell children would join her. Peter liked playing airplane and Joan usually was a Red Cross nurse who had to dig Una out of the ruins of a building; Patsy preferred to be a refugee who helped Una escape. It was a lovely game.

What Eunice liked best of all about her new life was being able to say "we" again. She had been a lonely "I" for so long, poor thing. She liked to put her arm through Mr. Spencer's and announce that:

"*We* like browned potatoes better than chips," or

"*We* like walking a lot, don't we Gramp?" or

"*We* love fairy tales best of all."

Gramp would smile and pat her hand and agree to everything. Eunice's health was improving so much that the doctor advised that she be sent to school. Of course Eunice wanted to go to Joan's school and Mr. Spencer had no objection to that. But Eunice couldn't be in Joan's class, nor even in Patsy's. Though she could read fairly well, she knew so little of other subjects that she had to start in first grade, but the teacher promised that, with a little help from her grandfather, she would be able to hop over to third grade after the summer holidays.

Peter was delighted to have her in his class. He took

good care of her, showing her where to put her books and hang her clothes and where the pencil sharpener was, helping her with her work and telling his friends that she had seen Real Germans and had been bombed, until she became the most popular person in the class. She was so small, she didn't look much taller than the other children.

And so the long months of January and February flashed past much quicker than usual. The Five for Victory Club languished a little in the cold weather, but Blinkie and Bertha provided a lot of amusement on dark, rainy days when the children couldn't go out. And as an added diversion a new pet entered the family. Andy's parents had moved out of the Haunted House and left a homeless kitten. It tried to get food out of garbage cans in the alley, but it was getting very thin and dirty and mewed a lot.

Eunice found it one day almost half dead on the door-

step of the Mitchell home and she brought it in, weeping over its bedraggled fur. Mother agreed that they couldn't let the poor thing die of want, so it was given a saucer of milk and a little basket to sleep in, and it became the sixth pet of the Mitchell household. Her name was Snow White, because that's what she got to look like when she had lived a while in her new home. Informally, however, she was usually called Kitty.

And so, what with one thing and another, winter ran its gray and misty course and spring was on the way again, sending snowdrops and crocuses and daffodils as advance guards. Mother began spading her victory garden, and Joan had to pull down her hut. She hated to do it, it had been so useful and Uncle Jim had made it so strong, but it couldn't be helped; Mother needed the space for vegetables. The Government was asking people not to give up their victory gardens as there would be great need of vegetables that year. But just as Joan was mourning her lost clubhouse, a wonderful thing happened. Peter discovered it first and came running to tell:

"Mrs. Trotter is going to leave! The White Elephant will be ours again!" he shouted.

"Are you sure?" cried Joan, unable to believe her good fortune.

"Come and look!" cried Peter.

It was true. Large moving vans were standing before the White Elephant's door and Mrs. Trotter was bustling in and out, giving directions in an excited voice. Henry leant languidly against a tree, chewing a blade of grass. He'd never been well since he'd had measles, he explained to Joan when she asked him what was happening.

"I had pneumonia and pleurisy," he said in a superior voice, as if it were rather clever of him to have illnesses with such long names. "This climate doesn't suit me. I need mountain air. We're going back to our home in the Adirondacks. It's tough luck on Mom," he added carelessly, running long fingers through his yellow hair, "but it suits me fine. Washington is too bureaucratic for me."

Joan looked at him with open mouth. She didn't like Henry, but he did know some wonderful words.

From that day the Mitchell children could hardly wait to take possession of their former paradise again. It was looking its prettiest now, with buds opening everywhere, spreading soft, green wings; crocuses pushing their colorful heads through the withered grass, jonquils blowing their yellow horns, and birds building nests in the comfortable old trees.

It was a good time for the club to go into action again. All the neighbors needed their yards cleared of rubbish, their paths raked, or their victory gardens spaded. Presently the Mitchell children had earned enough money to buy their bond, which they did with great solemnity.

Meanwhile Blinkie gave some trouble. He was feeling the spring. He was a large, handsome squirrel now and Bertha's company no longer satisfied him. He wanted to go out and see the world, and soon found a hole in the screen through which he crawled. Bertha didn't follow him. She was no climber and knew where she was well off. Blinkie stayed away for three days and then came back again, ravenously hungry and happy to dive into his old, warm little nest. Joan plugged up the hole in the screen, glad to have her pet back again.

The first thing almost which the Mitchell children had asked when they knew Mr. Spencer to be Eunice's grandfather was: "When is Eunice's birthday?"

Mr. Spencer had thought it over for a moment, and then

he had remembered perfectly. It was on the tenth of April, and this year she would be nine years old. Eunice was delighted. To have a birthday all her own seemed to her the most important thing in the world. It showed that she really and truly belonged somewhere; that she had a country of her own and a place where she had begun, like everybody else.

As the day drew near she grew more and more excited, and kept telling everybody how she wanted it celebrated. There was to be a dinner party, like grown-ups have, with soup and dessert. She also wanted a real evening dress, which fell down to your feet and had fluffy frills on it. It must on no account be either "sensible" or "practical." She had worn sensible and practical clothes for so long. She also wanted a doll so she could have her own child when she played house with Joan and Patsy and needn't borrow one from Angela. In fact, Eunice wanted so many things that it worried Joan.

"I'm afraid she'll be disappointed," she told Eunice's grandfather in confidence. "You know how it is. People want and want things and then, when they get them, they're not really happy, because they thought it would be quite different. I am like that. I am always wanting things." She sighed. "I wish I didn't. I wanted a pet and now I have six of them and it isn't what I wanted. Not a single one of them is what I wanted. You see, I really want a dog pet, a kind of pal. Of course Blinkie is a friend in a way, he sits on my shoulder and eats out of my hand, but I think he'd rather be up a tree with another squirrel. He used to like me best," said Joan wistfully, "when he needed me to give him food, but he can eat so well now, he can even crack those hard Brazil nuts with his own teeth. So you see, he could just as well be free, only I'd miss him so." She sighed again. "That's why I'd like a dog; a dog would rather be with me than with another dog, wouldn't he?"

"Yes, I think he would," agreed Mr. Spencer.

"But Daddy won't let me have a dog," Joan continued sadly. "And perhaps a dog would be a disappointment, too. The kitty was. She cares more for her milk than for anyone."

"Mew," said the kitty, rubbing herself against Joan's legs. Joan picked it up and held her cheek against its downy fur.

"I guess I'm ungrateful," she said.

"Hi ya, fellows, ain't it a terrible war?" croaked Mr. Jenkins, hopping on his perch. Joan laughed.

"They're fun all the same," she admitted. "Only . . . do people *ever* get what they want, Mr. Spencer?" Mr. Spencer looked at her, his blue eyes serene.

"Not until they're in Heaven," he said.

"I see." Joan gave another sigh. "It's a long time to wait, isn't it? And I *do* so want Eunice to be happy on her birthday."

"Oh, I think we can manage that all right," said Mr. Spencer comfortably. "If you'll help me." And Joan and he went into a long consultation.

On the morning of Eunice's birthday the sun shone golden through the windows. It promised to be a beautiful day. Patsy and Joan got up quietly, taking care not to wake Eunice, and tiptoed downstairs, where they decorated Eunice's chair with jonquils. Joan then dressed Timmy, who was a big boy now—almost two—and could say many words. Angela dressed herself. When they looked pretty enough to please Joan, they were allowed to go down and hold their presents. Mr. Spencer had already arrived in the dining room, in a new suit, bought especially for the occasion. (It was high time he had one, according to Grannie.)

Peter went to fetch Eunice, who came down shyly. She had found a new dress on the chair beside her bed. It wasn't the long dress she had asked for, but it looked pretty, sprinkled with flowers and with a ribbon around the waist. Eunice felt like a fairy.

"Happy birthday to you!" sang the children. Eunice blushed and accepted the presents that were showered on her.

"Thank you, oh *thank* you!" she kept saying. There was a doll with lovely clothes, a book, a box of crayons, a sketchbook and a big bag of candy with which to treat the children at school. But the best present was Grandfather's. It was the most beautiful long party dress a little girl ever had. The children all gasped at its shimmering folds of blue satin and tulle, sprinkled with silver stars. Joan was happy to see that Eunice was not a bit disappointed; her face glowed as if a candle had been lit behind it and she moved as if in a magic circle where no harm could reach her.

The afternoon party would be later than usual because it was to be a dinner. The children had been invited mostly by Joan, who told her mother that she had selected the "best-mannered" boys. They were truly well-behaved when they turned up, dressed in dark suits with clean collars, their hair slicked down on their heads.

The girls looked more frivolous in colorful, flouncy dresses, but none of them was as beautiful as Eunice in her glittering evening dress. After a while the excess of manners wore off a little, but only after the sliding doors had been opened, showing the prettily decorated table with its bowls of steaming soup, did the true fun start.

Not one of the children had ever been to a dinner party before, and a little girl got so excited she had to telephone her mother to inform her that "we're having *soup!!* "

The soup was such a novelty that it was eaten solemnly, with reverence. But at the second course of potato chips, salad and ham, the tongues came loose and wagged so merrily, they could be heard a block away.

When finally the magnificent cake appeared, with its nine burning candles, there was such singing and cheering that Eunice grew shy and ran to bury her face in her grandfather's waistcoat. She wasn't used to being the heroine of a party. But after a while she recovered and joined in the games which Joan started, looking so radiantly happy that Mr. Spencer got tears in his eyes watching her.

"It's been a real success," Mother told him when the last tired guest had departed, laden with favors and sweets.

"I almost think any party would have been a success with Eunice," said Mr. Spencer. "She was so conscious of the privilege of having a birthday that she spun her own happiness, like a little spider."

But the day was not to end joyfully after all. When Mother had put the children to bed and relaxed into a chair to rest, there was a ring at the door. Mother opened it and saw a messenger stand with a pile of yellow telegrams in his hand. Her heart started to beat fast and seemed to give a jump.

"What is it?" she asked.

"Telegram," said the messenger briefly.

"I thought they always sent them over the phone,"

faltered Mother. The messenger said nothing. Mother thought she had never seen such a gloomy-looking person.

"What is it?" asked Grannie, coming downstairs.

"Telegram," said Mother, a catch in her voice. Grannie stood motionless for a moment, one hand fluttering to her throat. Mother was ripping open the telegram with trembling fingers.

"Oh," she cried, and burst into tears. Grannie took the telegram from her.

"We regret to inform you that your husband, Lieutenant John Ruysdaal Mitchell, is missing in action," she read. The paper shook between her fingers.

"Please, ma'am," said a voice from the door. "You still got to sign this paper." Neither Mother nor Grannie seemed to be able to understand what the messenger wanted. At last Mr. Spencer came to the rescue and signed for them.

With a sigh the messenger took up his terrible burden and shuffled off on his unhappy mission, bringing sorrow and suffering to many households.

In the Mitchell home Mother and Grannie sat together, each trying to put hope into the other's heart, though her own was sorely troubled.

But the children slept, not knowing what evil tidings the night had brought them.

TWENTY

Anxious Days

THE next morning the children had to be informed of the bad news. Mother first told Peter when he had just woken up, dreams still lingering in his dark eyes, his hair tousled from the pillow.

"We learnt something very sad yesterday, my dear," she said, holding his hand. "Your daddy is missing in action." Peter looked at her solemnly, taking it in.

"I know," he nodded. "His ship was sunk. I've seen it in the movies. He'll be saved, though. Most of the people are saved. Perhaps he has a raft . . . or maybe he can *swim* home. Daddy is very good at swimming." Nothing could shake Peter's conviction that Daddy would be all right, and Mother envied him as she watched him go his lighthearted way. Joan and Patsy understood the gravity of the situation better, though they, too, were full of hope.

Eunice's heart overflowed with pity when she heard that Mr. Mitchell was missing. She put herself out to do little things for the various members of the family to console them. She laid a hot water bottle in Grannie's bed every night and took care that there was always a vase with fresh flowers on the dining room table. She also minded the little ones when she saw they were bothering the grown-ups.

There was a notice in the paper about Daddy, but it didn't give his full name. "Lieutenant J.R. Mitchell," it said, and soon afterward there was a ring at the door of the Mitchell house. As Mother opened the door, she saw none other than Yeoman Sullivan, who asked in a trembling voice:

"Is it . . . is it Jim?" For a moment Mother felt glad that she could say: "No, it's my husband." Yeoman Sullivan lowered her eyes to hide their sudden, glad radiance. "I am so sorry for you," she faltered, blushing. "You have my heartfelt sympathy."

"I know," said Mother softly. "Won't you come in?" Mary Sullivan said she would love to, and presently accepted a cup of coffee. She looked so kind and pretty that Mother didn't blame Uncle Jim for liking her. Apparently she liked Uncle Jim, too. She kept talking about him and at the end she wrote down his address.

"I'll have to tell him how sorry I am about his brother," she explained, but she didn't look so sorry at that moment.

Mother smiled a little as she watched Yeoman Sullivan

skip down the steps again, looking ten years younger than when she had come up.

Mother had often noticed that troubles are like grapes, they come in bunches. When she told Cora about the telegram Cora was very distressed.

"Oh, and that it should have happened just now, when I have to leave you, ma'am!" she cried.

"Leave us?" said Mother, alarmed.

"Yes, ma'am, my husband has got a defense job in Detroit, and I've got to go with him. I hate leaving you all, especially now this has happened to Mr. Mitchell."

Mother sat perfectly still for a moment. "Well, it can't be helped," she sighed. "I wish you the best of luck, Cora."

After this piece of news Mother tried to find another servant, but all the agencies said they had more calls than they could fill.

So Joan called a special meeting of the club in the White Elephant's playhouse, to discuss the matter. Mother had been invited, too, and Joan opened the meeting solemnly.

"This is a very important occasion because my mother wants to say something," she announced. "And anyone who doesn't pay attention can do without refreshments," she ended severely. There was an immediate silence.

"I've got to keep them in order," Joan told Mother in a whisper. "They're only kids, you know." Then, loudly:

"Members, here is Mrs. Mitchell." Mother stood up and bowed and the children all clapped.

"Thank you," said Mother. "I am very grateful for the opportunity to talk to you. When Joan first told me that she was going to start a club to help us win the war, I thought, well at any rate it can do no harm! But since then

I have watched with admiration how you have worked together, and have conquered many difficulties that were thrown into your way. Seeing you in action has given me faith in the future of our country."

The children clapped loudly, blushing with delight at Mother's praise.

"Now I want to ask your help," she went on. "Cora has left us and it will be hard for me to manage unless you do your share. If you each undertake to do some of the work and keep it up faithfully, I promise to give you four war stamps every week to paste into your new stampbook."

"Hurrah!" cried the children.

Joan now handed round the refreshments and proposed that they should parcel out the tasks each member had to do.

Peter said he'd do the messages, polish the shoes, make his own bed and vacuum clean the floor. Patsy, after a struggle with herself, promised to wash the dishes, hoping she would be able to do so with a book propped up against the wall. Eunice said she'd lay the table for meals and keep the girls' room tidy, and Joan undertook to help with the laundry and to keep the kitchen and bathrooms scrubbed.

"But I, what shall I do?" asked Dickie, who hated to be left out.

"You can help me run errands," said Peter, "and you can bring things to the salvage and clean up rubbish in the yard. I won't have time for that sort of thing any more," he added loftily.

The children worked hard the first days after Cora had left, and they were learning as well as helping. It was one thing to make a mess when Cora was there; quite another when you had to clean it up yourselves. Also, Joan soon told Peter he'd have to stop wiping his dirty hands on the towels, since she had to do the simple laundry. So a kind of self-discipline crept into the Mitchell family which gladdened Mother's heart. It needed to be gladdened, for it was heavy with anxiety and sorrow. What was to become of the many little Mitchells should their father never return? Day after day went past without further news, and gradually Mother's hope that Daddy might yet be picked up out of the sea oozed away. The children, too, sensed the threat that hung over their lives, though they tried not to think of it. Fear would clutch them suddenly, in the middle of a game, like a dark hand squeezing their hearts.

"Surely no one could stand being on a raft this long. . . ." Mother said to Grannie, when a week had dragged itself past.

But the children were sure that God would hear their prayers, and it was their confidence which somehow kept hope alive in Mother's and Grannie's hearts.

One afternoon Mother stood watching some birds that were pecking at the crumbs Timmy had spilt on the porch. She was thinking about Daddy and how sad and empty the future would be without him, and praying that he might yet be saved, when the second telegram came: the lovely, the beautiful telegram which told that Daddy had been found, that he was alive and would come home soon. Mother ran into the house, shouting her delight. The children crowded around her, wanting to hear all about it, but Mother was in Grannie's arms and to the children's amazement they both burst into tears.

"Aren't you *glad?*" asked Peter indignantly.

"Of course I am, my darling," said Mother, embracing as many of her children as she could gather in her arms. "Of course I am, terribly, terribly grateful and glad. But

I've been swallowing so many tears the last days, they just
have to come out first before I can laugh again!"

A few hours later a third telegram came. Mother and
Grannie were afraid to open it. What if it said that the
other one had been a mistake, that it was a Lieutenant
Michael who had been found instead? That would be too
cruel. At last Grannie summoned sufficient courage to tear
it open.

"It's from Jim!" she cried jubilantly. "They're both on
leave, they're coming here as soon as John is discharged
from the hospital. They'll be with us for Easter! Oh, Rita,
John was found by his brother, his own brother saved
him. . . ." And to the children's bewilderment Mother
and Grannie forsook their new-found smiles and burst
into fresh tears.

It seemed that Uncle Jim had found Daddy drifting on a raft and had, at great risk, alighted to take him on board his plane.

"There now," said Joan. "If Uncle Jim had stayed home like you wanted him to, Patsy, we'd have lost Daddy." Mother wiped her eyes.

"And now," she cried, "we're going to clean the house."

"And kill the fatted calf, eh, Mother?" observed Joan mischievously.

TWENTY-ONE

Daddy Comes Home

O N THE Saturday before Easter, Mother was so ex-cited she couldn't think. She really didn't know how she would have managed without Joan and the Club. There was Easter to think of as well as the men coming home; there had to be a delicious dinner which would have to be prepared beforehand. The house had to be cleaned, the children's best clothes had to be ironed, and then there was the yard. Daddy simply *hated* a dirty yard and Timmy kept scattering papers over it. And then there was the wall along the staircase. It showed the marks of dirty little hands all the way up. It really should be painted. Mother was frantic. She ran around with a red face, shouted at the children, started to do one thing, dropped it for another thing, dropped that for a third, until the children and Grannie got dizzy just looking at her.

"I do wish you wouldn't fuss so, Rita," Grannie advised gently. "It's *you* John wants to see, not the house!"

"Yes, but he likes things to be neat and I'm *not* going to disappoint him," said Mother fiercely. "Perfection is not too good for him—it's been *so* long!" Mother almost began to weep again, and Joan realized it was time someone took the situation in hand. She was eleven now and a big girl.

"You're not going to do all that work today, Mother," she said firmly. "I know exactly what would happen if you did. You'd be dead tired tomorrow and you wouldn't be able to enjoy Daddy. You leave the whole thing to us. You ought to go downtown to have your hair done; you look much worse than the house."

Mother gazed at her eldest daughter in amazement. She hadn't realized how much Joan had grown lately.

"But you kids can't do all that . . . ," she began.

"Yes, we can," said Joan. "You'll see. We want to do it for you," she pleaded. "I know we're often a lot of bother and I guess we can't help that, but we'd like to show you what we can do because we love you very much, Mother, and Daddy, too. The trouble with mothers is," Joan went on wisely, "that they never give you a *chance* to be nice to them, they're too unselfish." Joan's face, as she coaxed Mother, was very sweet: pink and confident and full of shy affection.

"Well . . . ," began Mother. She *had* thought that her hair needed curling and of course John *did* love it when she looked pretty—it would be wonderful to have a day off...

"What do you think?" she asked of Grannie. Grannie smiled.

"Go, by all means," she said. "I've got faith in those youngsters of yours." Joan gave Grannie a grateful smile and Grannie nodded at her. She'd be there still to give advice and direction when Joan needed it.

So it was decided that Mother would go out. She departed in high spirits, waved off by her brood.

"Thank goodness," sighed Joan. "Now we'll have peace at last." Grannie laughed.

"You'd better do some work, too," she advised. "You undertook rather a lot, you know."

"Just watch us," said Joan.

Grannie did watch them and she was pleased. Without bossing, Joan had her club in full control, inspiring its members with her enthusiasm.

Even Angela caught the spirit of the thing. She washed all her dolls' clothes and made a house for Traincrack out of some chairs. Surshy she put to sleep in Daddy's old hat, and she covered the floor with little pieces of paper which were meant for dishes, on which she put raisins for food. She looked forward to showing this beautiful arrangement to an admiring Daddy, but unfortunately Patsy had different ideas. She had been assigned to do the bedrooms and she did Angela's thoroughly, sweeping away all the "trash." When Angela discovered this she was indignant.

"How can I keep my room neat when you keep messing it up all the time," she told Patsy severely.

Joan found some paint in the cellar and decided to start on the wall. But unfortunately Timmy fell in the bucket of paint and had to be put in the bathtub to soak for a while. He enjoyed this very much and amused himself by squirting water all over the floor. But Joan said that was a help because she had to scrub the floor anyway.

Joan really was a wonder. After she had painted the wall, not the whole wall but the strip that was dirty, she polished the floors and made the beds, putting Eunice in her grandfather's room so Angela could sleep with her sisters and Uncle Jim could have Angela's room.

She also took care of Timmy and kept him out of mischief. Peter and Dickie did the shopping. Mother had told them what to get before she left.

Eunice polished the furniture and picked jonquils in the White Elephant's yard, arranging them tastefully in vases. Patsy swept the rugs. She swept some of the dirt under the chairs because she didn't think Daddy would look there, but the general effect was clean.

Grannie showed Angela how to polish silver and let her help lay the table for dinner. Mother wouldn't be there, she was going to eat out. Grannie treated the children to their favorite hot dogs with lots of mustard, peanut butter sandwiches, and jellied doughnuts. After dinner, the whole club went to clean up the yard. Even Timmy helped, and he found his silver mug which had been lost for three weeks. Patsy sang as she raked up the dry grass. Then she rested awhile, leaning on the rake handle.

"I am *so* glad Daddy is coming back," she sighed. "I wish he could be back forever. I wish the war were over."

"It must be over some time," Peter observed thoughtfully, putting down his basket of trash for a moment. "They've been shooting so many enemies there can't be many more left, do you think?"

"What *I'm* scared of," said Joan, throwing another scrap

of paper in Peter's basket, "is that Daddy will be mad with us."

"Why?" the children were startled.

"Because of our pets," said Joan. "He'll probably think it's a zoo here and he *told* me not to get a lot of animals in the house." Joan really looked worried. "I should *hate* to have Daddy angry the first day he is home."

"Why don't we *hide* them?" asked Patsy. "Then he won't see them right away and we can make him get used to them one by one."

"Yes, but *where?*" asked Joan.

"I know a place!" cried Peter. He whispered something in Joan's ear. Joan nodded.

"Anyway, we can set Blinkie free," she said. "He wants to be free so badly it is unfair to keep him in the porch." So Blinkie was put at liberty, all the children watching as he scurried up a tree.

"That's one," said Joan. "Now the others." They went around the house, whispering mysteriously. "We'll have to do it tomorrow," said Joan, "first thing."

When Mother came home she couldn't believe her eyes. The house looked as clean as if Cora were still there and all that was left for her to do was to bake a ham and a couple of pies and help the children wash their hair. Mother looked lovely herself with curls and shiny nails and eyes so bright they put the stars to shame. The children felt proud of her. She had bought herself a new hat too, without cherries this time, and a dress with a pretty flowered pattern all over.

"I've had a grand time," she said, kissing her children. "Thank you so much, darlings, you've been *wonderful!*" And that was reward enough for anyone.

A song seemed to be echoing through the house.

"Daddy is coming home, Daddy is coming home." The clock was saying it and the teakettle. The wind was whispering it down the chimney. The shining floors smiled it, the lamps beamed it, and if you listened to the beats of your heart they were saying it, too.

"Daddy is coming home! Daddy is coming home!" How could anyone sleep listening to such a song? But the morning came at last, Easter morning with the sun shining on a gay breakfast table and six little Easter baskets filled with candy. The children had painted a dozen hard-boiled eggs, too, and they added to the cheerful effect.

"Easter is lovely," remarked Peter. "But I'm more excited about Daddy coming home."

The others agreed with him. The girls wore pretty dresses and Peter had put on his white suit, but while he was waiting to go to church he slid down the grassy slope a couple of times and after that it wasn't so white any more.

The children wondered whether Daddy had arrived when they came home after church, but he hadn't yet. The dinner was ready and waiting: a spicy ham, baked sweet potatoes, salad with colorful eggs on it, cauliflower, applesauce, and Daddy's favorite pie for dessert. It was all getting cold and yet there was no Daddy.

Mother felt worried.

"He said he'd be here at twelve," she remarked again and again. "Go and watch out for him."

The children were all looking through the hall window when Daddy and Jim entered the house by the back door.

"Hey, is nobody home to welcome a shipwrecked sailor?" they cried.

Then, of course, they got it from all sides. The children ran shrieking through the hall to meet them, Grannie flung her arms around Uncle Jim and Mother hugged

Daddy to pieces. There was no end to the exclamations and confusions as all the little Mitchells clamored for attention.

Daddy looked thin and haggard. As he said, eight days on a raft are no beauty treatment. But he was full of admiration for his wife and children.

"Rita, you look as young as when I married you," he told his wife. "How do you manage it?"

"I guess the children manage it for me," said Mother, winking at Joan, who was as proud of Daddy's compliment as if it had been paid to herself.

Daddy said all his children looked fine, but he couldn't get over Timmy.

"The boy is a *giant!*" he exclaimed. "He'll be a prizefighter one day!" Then he stroked Angela's curls.

"Is this little girl as naughty as ever?" he asked.

"No, she is good now," Joan assured him. "I've been training her."

"Well, well, and you're quite a young lady now, Joan. I bet you're a help to your mother. And Peter! My goodness, he'll grow to be six feet. And Patsy doesn't look as dreamy as she did. Is that Una?"

"Eunice," Joan corrected him.

"How did you know about me?" asked Eunice shyly, shaking Daddy by the hand.

"Oh, Joan wrote me," smiled Daddy. "I had Joan's last letter in my pocket when our ship was sunk. It was all I had to read during those days on the raft and believe me, I know it by heart now. Thanks for writing such long letters, Joanie."

"Oh, tell us about your shipwreck, Daddy!" cried Peter. "Did you get wet?"

"Did I get wet?" Daddy laughed heartily. "You don't

get wet in a nice, dry, tidy ocean. What are you thinking of?"

"But . . ." said Peter, looking bewildered. "I thought . . ."

"You thought the sea was wet, eh?" said Father. "Well, you're right, son, I was only teasing you. I got so wet I didn't know what was my inside and what was my outside any more." The children thought this very funny, though Daddy assured them it didn't *feel* funny at all.

"My goodness, I was glad to get on that raft," he said. "But I was even gladder to get off it. When I saw Jim I went almost crazy with happiness. You get a little crazy anyway, sitting alone on a raft without any protection against sun and rain, with only the sea around you and the wind in your ears. I thought I was dreaming when I saw Jim's plane."

"You weren't more amazed than I was," said Uncle Jim. "I still think it was a miracle I found you. If I hadn't got a little off my course, I'd have missed you completely. And I don't think you could have held out much longer."

"No, Jim saved my life all right," said Daddy, putting a hand on Uncle Jim's shoulder. "And then he brought me to a hospital and asked leave to bring me home as soon as I was well enough to go."

"Oh, *thank* you, Uncle Jim, *thank* you," cried Patsy, rubbing her cheek against Uncle Jim's coat.

"Listen," cried Mother from the dining room. "This dinner has been sitting here too long already; come and eat!"

"Better words were never spoken," cried Uncle Jim, striding ahead of the others. It was a lovely meal. Daddy and Uncle Jim kept praising the food and Mother beamed. Meanwhile Timmy provided entertainment. He was too excited to eat. He took the plate of food Mother had set before him, cried "Up he goes!" and threw it into the air. It came down with a bang, scattering applesauce in all directions. Mother scolded Timmy, but Timmy was not impressed.

"It's funny," he chortled, dimpling all over. Alas for discipline, Daddy and Uncle Jim were shaking with laughter.

It was a lovely warm day and the windows were open, though the screens hadn't been put in yet. Suddenly, to Daddy's open-mouthed wonder, a squirrel hopped through one of them and made himself at home in the dining room. He tried to find a pleasant spot to eat a peanut and Daddy seemed the likeliest person to explore. He ran up Daddy's trousers, jumped on his shoulder, and from there to his head, where he squatted on Daddy's thinning hair and began to eat his peanut, dropping the shell on Daddy's nose.

The children almost fell off their chairs with laughter, but Daddy remained quite calm.

"Is he a friend of yours?" he asked, but then he sneezed, having sniffed up a piece of peanutshell. Blinkie didn't like the sound of that sneeze and went to sit in Uncle Jim's pocket instead, where Uncle Jim fed him tidbits from the table.

"Well, is he, atchoo, atchoo, a friend of yours?" repeated Father.

"Yes," admitted Joan, blushing a little. "Yes, he is a friend of ours."

"His name is Blinkie," volunteered Angela.

"Ha, Blinkie," said Daddy, looking mysterious. "You don't have a *dog* by any chance, do you?" he asked, fixing a piercing glance on his eldest daughter.

"Oh no, no, Daddy, we really haven't," Joan assured him quickly. "We know you hate them."

"Fine," murmured Daddy, with a sly look at Uncle Jim. Uncle Jim took a big drink, but it went down the wrong hole and he choked. All the children got up to pat him on the back. It was hard for Uncle Jim to stop them once they got going, and Daddy had to come to the rescue and send the children back to their chairs.

Daddy had finished eating and was lighting his pipe when he listened for a moment.

"Hush," he said. "I think I hear rats. Have you got rats here?" There was a queer scratchy noise inside the buffet. Daddy opened one of its doors and out jumped a fat gray rabbit.

"Oh my goodness!" cried Daddy. "What an enormous rat!"

"It isn't a rat!" shrieked the children. "It's Eunice's bunny!"

"I see." Daddy looked at it as it hopped through the room. "Why do you keep it in the buffet?" he asked.

"Oh, we were just hiding it," confessed Patsy. "Because you hate animals."

"Well, you don't have to hide it any more," observed Daddy. "Take it where it belongs before it lays an egg on the sofa."

The children protested.

"Bunnies don't *lay eggs!* "

"Not even for Easter?" asked Daddy. "I don't trust it. Take it away!"

Peter went off to bring Bertha back to the porch, and Daddy followed Uncle Jim and the ladies into the living room, where Mother poured out coffee.

Daddy was just going to drink some when a sound startled him.

"Don't fret," came a voice from the chimney. "Everything will be OK."

"My goodness," said Daddy. "Who on earth is *that?* It's *much* too early for Santa Claus."

"Happy birthday to you," said the same voice.

"Same to you," Daddy answered politely. He was on his hands and knees now and gazed up the chimney.

"Meet Mr. Jenkins," said the bird politely. His cage was hanging inside the chimney on a nail. Daddy unhooked it.

"Well, well! Look what Santa Claus brought me and it isn't even Christmas!" he said. "He must have heard that lots of servicemen celebrate it around this time of the year. Hello, Mr. Jenkins."

Mr. Jenkins watched Daddy with his head to one side, a melancholy expression on his face.

"Ain't this a terrible war?" he murmured sadly. Daddy laughed and put down the cage.

"Come one, come all," he cried. "The more the merrier." And he winked at Uncle Jim. The children were glad he wasn't angry and they hoped their other hiding places would remain undiscovered for a while, but luck was against them. Daddy wanted to light his pipe, dropped a match, and groped for it under the sofa.

"Ouch, what's this?" he cried, pulling back his hand which dripped with water. "What have you got under there?" And, bending down, he discovered the fishbowl.

"Stranger and stranger," he muttered. "What is this? A conspiracy? I hope you haven't got a lion or tiger hidden somewhere."

"Mew! Mew!" said a little voice behind the cellar door.

"Aha!" cried Daddy and went to open it. Out tripped Snow White, rubbing her head against Daddy's legs.

"Now look here, this can't go on . . . ," began Daddy, but the children all assured him in chorus that there wasn't a single pet hidden anywhere any more.

"Are you *positive?*" asked Daddy.

"Oh *yes!*" cried the children.

"What will you bet?" asked Daddy.

"If you find a single other animal we'll each give you our best Easter egg," promised Joan. "But if you don't you'll have to give us one."

"All right," said Daddy. "Go and look in the garage, Joan."

"B-but . . . ," stammered Joan.

"Go ahead, look in the garage," said Daddy. There was a mysterious expression on his face. The children all ran outside. There were queer noises in the garage.

"Perhaps Daddy has brought us a baby orphan after all," whispered Patsy.

"How could he, from the sea? It's more likely to be a mermaid or a baby whale," argued Joan.

She cautiously opened the door of the garage, holding her breath. Then she was almost knocked over by a little black and white dog, who jumped up at her, barking furiously.

"A dog! A dog! Oh! A dog!" cried Joan rapturously, folding the creature in her arms. Then her face fell.

"What will Daddy say?"

"Daddy won't say anything," cried Uncle Jim, who was standing on the back porch, his hands in his pockets and a grin on his face. "He's Daddy's dog."

"*Daddy's* dog? But . . ."

"You lost the bet!" cried Daddy, stepping up beside Uncle Jim. "You all owe me an Easter egg."

"Do you mean . . . do you mean we're going to keep him?" asked Joan incredulously.

"I wouldn't part with him," said Daddy firmly. "He was my only friend for eight days. You see, he was the ship's mascot and he alone managed to climb on the raft with me. He has no master any more, poor thing, and if it hadn't been for him I wouldn't have been alive when Uncle Jim found me. He kept my courage up, didn't you, Trusty?" And Daddy took the little dog in his arms and fondled it.

The children at first could hardly believe their eyes. Then they whooped and cheered and made Trusty feel thoroughly at home.

"Well, who'd have thought that, John," said Mother, when the children had introduced her to the new pet. "For you to bring a dog into the house."

Daddy laughed.

"That's why I hid him in the garage," he explained. "I was afraid you wouldn't believe it was I if I walked in with a dog. . . . "

The children now romped with Trusty, leaving their father and uncle some peace. Daddy stretched himself out on the sofa; he still felt very weak. Uncle Jim said he had to make a call and would be back soon. Presently he returned, walking arm and arm with Yeoman Sullivan. They both looked as happy as children on a merry-go-round.

"Congratulate me, everybody," Uncle Jim shouted the minute he was in the house. "Meet the future Mrs. Jim Mitchell!"

"Jim! Is it true!" cried Grannie, kissing Mary Sullivan, who blushed shyly.

"Of course it's true, what else?" cried Uncle Jim boisterously. "She doesn't know yet what a bad bargain she has made, so don't go telling on me now, I don't want to lose her." And he looked at his promised wife with his whole heart in his eyes.

"Oh, Jim, I'm so glad," said Mother. "You *do* need a wife, and he'll be a good husband, too, Mary, only you'll have to teach him not to throw ashes around.

"Oh hush," protested Uncle Jim, blushing. "Don't go telling tales now."

Daddy had got up from the couch and now shook hands with Mary Sullivan, too.

"I've heard a lot about you," he said. "Jim couldn't talk of anything else."

"Oh hush," said Uncle Jim, blushing more than ever. The children saved him this time; they were much more interested in the details of a wedding than in anyone's emotions.

"Will you be a bride with a veil?" Patsy asked of Mary.

"May we be bridesmaids?" begged Joan.

"Me, too?" asked Eunice.

"You may all be bridesmaids and Peter could be a page," promised Mary Sullivan, who looked as if she would have granted anybody anything, she was so happy.

"But Timmy then?" asked Angela.

"Oh, he can be Cupid," said Uncle Jim. "The costume is simple. Just a bow and arrows, that's all."

There was true happiness in the Mitchell family that evening. Grannie lit her fire because it had got chilly again, and they all sat around it, eating candy and popcorn. There was a little wine, too, for the grown-ups. Mr. Spencer had come in and sat in an easy chair, with Eunice on his lap. Uncle Jim had put a chair close to Mary Sullivan's, and he was holding her hand. Mother and Daddy sat together on the couch and Grannie had Timmy, who was fast asleep, on her lap. Angela had crawled on Daddy's knee and was almost asleep herself, blinking drowsily and contentedly about her. Peter and Patsy sat on a bench in front of the fire and traded eggs out of their baskets, while Joan sat way back in a big chair with Trusty. It seemed like Heaven to have a dog at last, and Trusty loved her already, she could see that. Of course, her troubles weren't over forever; Daddy and Uncle Jim would have to go back to the war again with all its hazards and some day Eunice and Mr. Spencer would have to return to their own country, but that was all so very far off still. Now everything was perfect. And Joan gave a sigh of deep content.

About the Author

Hilda van Stockum was born in Rotterdam, Holland, in 1908, daughter of a Dutch naval officer and an Irish-Dutch mother from whom she early learned English. Storytelling, art, fun and home-schooling (until age 10) enriched her young days. Her first plan was to become an artist. At age 16, having moved to Ireland with her family, she attended the School of Art in Dublin; later, the Dutch Academy in Amsterdam. Writing frequent letters to her mother (between Ireland and Holland), she developed her descriptive skills which would blossom into a career of distinction, writing and illustrating children's books.

Those books began immediately after her marriage to an American, Ervin Marlin, in 1932, and continued over a 43-year period to roll from her pen. *A Day on Skates*, set in Holland, helped pay her way to America. Other early books captured life in Ireland. But soon the years of marriage and motherhood to six young Marlins offered a fresh field for good story and good humor. *The Mitchells: Five for Victory* draws directly from her family life with growing children, as do its sequels, *Canadian Summer* and *Friendly Gables*. Empathy with children and an instinct for the importance of small things characterize these and all Miss van Stockum's works. As her children grew up, Miss van Stockum took inspiration from other sources, returning, in some tales, both to Holland and Ireland and venturing even to Africa. The Marlins settled eventually in England to be near three daughters and numerous grandchildren. Today, Mrs. Marlin (Hilda van Stockum) continues to wield a paintbrush that fully justifies the renown she earned in her *other* career as artist.

Canadian Summer
by Hilda van Stockum

The Mitchells are leaving Washington D. C. The war is over and Daddy's work is moving the family—expanded now to include baby Catherine—to Canada. However, he hasn't been able to find a decent house in Montreal. Mother and Grannie arrive with the children to find that the only available housing is a remote summer cottage. What more could six healthy children want beyond a lake and a forest and a little camping? What less could Mother and Grannie wish than a primitive, isolated cabin from which to keep track of six city children? And Daddy comes home only on the weekends! Needless to say, an unforgettable summer unfolds for the Mitchell clan.

Friendly Gables
by Hilda van Stockum

Still in Canada, the Mitchells have now settled into a new home. Grannie has died, but *twins* have been added to the family. The children are growing up and their development is displayed against the backdrop of these changes in the household. With the twins has come a temporary nurse who is not at all as easy-going as Mother. With Mother recovering from the birth and harder to approach, the children must come to terms with themselves in a new way. Joan's first dance; what happens to Patsy when she loses her glasses; Peter's disastrous fight; Angela's misadventure in the woods; Timmy's "good news" and his new girl friend; and Catherine's brush with fire—make up only a fraction of the incidents in the life of this busy, growing family. With her usual humor and compassion, the author brings the Mitchell "trilogy" to a satisfying close.